D1536294

SPECIAL MESSAGE TO READERS

This book is published under the auspices of
THE ULVERSCROFT FOUNDATION
(registered charity No. 264873 UK)

Established in 1972 to provide funds for research, diagnosis and treatment of eye diseases. Examples of contributions made are: —

A new Children's Assessment Unit at
Moorfield's Hospital, London.

•

Twin operating theatres at the
Western Ophthalmic Hospital, London.

•

A Chair of Ophthalmology at the
University of Leicester.

•

The establishment of a Royal Australian College
of Ophthalmologists "Fellowship".

You can help further the work of the Foundation by making a donation or leaving a legacy. Every contribution, no matter how small, is received with gratitude. Please write for details to:

**THE ULVERSCROFT FOUNDATION,
The Green, Bradgate Road, Anstey,
Leicester LE7 7FU, England.
Telephone: (0116) 236 4325**

**In Australia write to:
THE ULVERSCROFT FOUNDATION,
c/o The Royal Australian College of
Ophthalmologists,
27, Commonwealth Street, Sydney,
N.S.W. 2010.**

LAREDO'S LAND

Laredo was the only man ever to escape from the infamous Mexican prison called Rebano. All he wanted was his land, but they'd stolen that while he was in that hell-hole. So he set out to take back what was his. Old friends became enemies and strangers became friends. Laredo would walk his land once again — or die trying. And he'd take a lot of men with him if he went down.

C.1

JAKE DOUGLAS

◆

LAREDO'S LAND

Complete and Unabridged

Bladen County Public Library
Elizabethtown, N. C. 28337

LINFORD
Leicester

First published in Great Britain in 1996 by
Robert Hale Limited
London

First Linford Edition
published 1997
by arrangement with
Robert Hale Limited
London

The right of Jake Douglas to be identified as
the author of this work has been asserted by
him in accordance with the
Copyright, Designs and Patents Act, 1988

Copyright © 1996 by Jake Douglas
All rights reserved

British Library CIP Data

Douglas, Jake
  Laredo's land.—Large print ed.—
  Linford western library
  1. Western stories
  2. Large type books
  I. Title
  823.9'14 [F]

  ISBN 0–7089–5125–2

Published by
F. A. Thorpe (Publishing) Ltd.
Anstey, Leicestershire

Set by Words & Graphics Ltd.
Anstey, Leicestershire
Printed and bound in Great Britain by
T. J. International Ltd., Padstow, Cornwall

This book is printed on acid-free paper

For
David, Matt and Ben —
A Great Guy!
*Muchas gracias,
amigo!*

1

THE sound of the firing squad echoed through the thick adobe walls of Rebano prison outside Hermisillo in the Sonora Province of Mexico, and Laredo began to relax. That ought to be all the excitement for the day, except for the cockroach race scheduled for noon after the slop they served for lunch.

But he was wrong. Although the sound of the firing squad had told him it was Thursday, booted feet coming down the stone corridor towards his cell set his heart racing. He listened as the sound came nearer, counting the steps of the marching guards — after almost five years in this corner of hell, he was able to tell just where they were in the passage by the number of steps.

Seventeen brought them to the cell of

el Loco Lobo, a man who was due to hang but his sentence had been passed three years ago. For Commandante Emilio Menendez was a man who prided himself on his 'humour' so he kept putting off the hanging day. The Wolf, a child killer, had been as sane as such a man could be when he had arrived at Rebano — which meant 'the herd' and Menendez treated his prisoners as he would a herd of wild animals — but now The Wolf had been driven completely out of his head with the strain of waiting.

The guards passed *Lobo*'s cell and Esperandas', and now was approaching Albano's. Next was the corner.

And the only cell after that was Laredo's.

They were coming for him.

He sighed and his knuckles whitened through the filth where he gripped the bars. Another few lashes were due to him today, it seemed . . .

After his capture and without a trial he had been sentenced to ten years in Rebano — which in itself was crass stupidity because no one had lasted past seven years in that hell-hole — yeah, ten years, plus fifty lashes.

But the considerate Commandante Emilio Menendez did not administer them all at once. Oh, no. His fun would be over too quickly.

So, he had started with ten lashes, the knotted rawhide whip crisscrossing Laredo's back and laying bare his ribs and a section of spine. Traditionally, salt had been rubbed into the wounds — to avoid infection, of course — but Menendez had stood by to watch the writhing and screaming.

Just as the weals were healing and Laredo was beginning to work without too much pain in the quarry, they came again in the cold dark hours one morning, dragged him into the whipping yard where Menendez, resplendent in his brown uniform, carefully pleated, boots polished, badges shining, waited beside the whipper,

El Latigo, smiling around his long, thick cigar.

"Ah, *amigo*, did you think I had forgotten you? Did you, perhaps, think I was being lenient, and going to forget that I owe you forty lashes . . . ? Ah, I am sorry, *mi amigo*, it is not possible. The paperwork, you know. It must show that you received your full quota. So, today I give you some more. We will try — five? *Si*, five."

Hatred glaring redly in his mattery eyes, Laredo was lashed up to the post, Menendez nodded, and *El Latigo* laid on the five in his usual crisscross pattern, avoiding the scars from the previous whipping, giving him a whole new network.

Each blow with the curling lash smashed the breath from his lungs and slammed his half-starved, though muscle-ridged body against the bloodstained post.

He was barely conscious when they cut him down, but he heard Menendez clearly enough.

"We will give him some more at a future time — I enjoy not knowing just when. I will make my decision" — he snapped his dark manicured fingers — "and then we will see how many more strokes I would like you to give him. Oh, and after the fiftieth, you will put out his left eye. With the lash. It can be done?"

"Of course, *commandante*. I will practise with your permission . . . ?"

There were now eleven prisoners in Rebano with only one eye.

And, after all this time, Laredo was due only three more lashes.

So today was to be the day when he would lose an eye.

The hell it was . . .

It was the usual squad of sadists, their boredom about to be relieved by his whipping and mutilation. Four of them, armed, sweaty, grinning in anticipation of his ordeal.

He didn't resist any more than usual. Let them think he had lost count of the strokes he had received with the whip.

Let them think he did not know he was about to have an eye put out with the silver tips *El Latigo* had crimped on to the rawhide thongs.

Let them think they were going to have an enjoyable morning, watching with *El Commandante*, as the whip was laid across his back which by now was a mass of scars, like a layer of dead purple and white snakes.

Yeah, let them drag him while he slumped between them as they spoke their rapid Spanish, too quickly for him to savvy, but he got the general gist of it.

Now here they were at the heavy, studded door that sealed off the whipping yard from the rest of the prison. An oblong, three yards by five, the worn, blood-soaked hardwood post standing with its shackles ready a yard from one of the narrow walls that was also spotted with dark blood and pieces of blackened flesh. *El Latigo* stood against the wall, smoking, his beloved whip coiled over one shoulder.

The silver tips glinted dully.

El Commandante stood back in the shade at the far end, resplendent as usual, his cigar burning well, adding its rich aroma to the stench of the whipping yard.

He smiled at Laredo, a figure in rags, lean, but hard-muscled from work in the quarry, his beard halfway down his chest, his lice-ridden hair hanging greasily past his shoulders. And out of the dark, lined face, the eyes blazed defiantly.

Menendez paused with his cigar halfway to his mouth, then gestured for the squad to bring Laredo before him. They dragged the man to stand a yard in front of the *commandante*. *El Latigo* relaxed, smoked his own foul-smelling cheroot. Menendez stepped close to Laredo.

"Ah, Texan, this is the last time we meet here. Unless, of course, you do something foolish that angers me and then I may have to add another fifty lashes to your sentence." He laughed and the others laughed dutifully.

Laredo said nothing.

Then Menendez drew deeply on his cigar and, surprising everyone there, reversed it and offered the wet end to Laredo.

"Taste some real tobacco, *amigo*. Instead of the straw and shit you smoke in the cell block. I am feeling generous today, and you know why . . . ? No? Because I know you are about to give me much pleasure. So, in my generosity, I will reward you before you perform for me, eh?"

He thrust the cigar closer and Laredo ran a tongue over his cracked lips, looked into Menendez's crazy eyes and reached for the cigar. As he had expected, the *commandante* pulled it just out of reach.

Then Laredo acted.

He drove the heel of his calloused hand against the butt of the cigar, smashing the red, burning end into Menendez's face. The man screamed as the searing coal was crushed against his olive skin, just beneath his left eye. While he was writhing and moaning and the others were too stunned to move, in those few seconds, Laredo had the *commandante*'s pistol, a huge French Le Mat with an extra barrel that held a shot-gun shell beneath the usual rifled barrel, and he slammed it against the side of Menendez's head, driving him to his knees. The first of the squad to lunge in, bringing up his Snider bolt-action rifle, lost the top of his head and the heavy ·40 calibre bullet went on to rip open the face of the man behind it until it ricocheted from the wall above *El Latigo*, who dropped hurriedly to his knees. Laredo pressed the selector button on the front of the frame.

The remaining members of the guard squad were cut down by the blast from the shot shell, one dead, the other writhing and bleeding on the ground.

El Latigo had uncoiled his whip and was swinging his arm back to deliver his blow when Laredo shot him through the left eye. His gore smeared the adobe wall as he slumped to the ground. He still had seven ·40 calibre shots left.

By that time, Laredo had Menendez on his feet, dazed and trying to hold the ugly burn on his face. The Texan drove the hot muzzle against his temple, the metal burning a brown ring through the short, oily hair.

"Now listen, Menendez," Laredo said in English — Menendez could speak perfect English but insisted that every prisoner learn Spanish to his satisfaction under pain of punishment. "We're getting out of here, you and me. One false move and I'll start shooting you to pieces. Oh, I won't kill you outright — not yet. That'd be crazy, but you could try getting along without an ear, or a hand, or a knee cap — or something more dear to you."

He moved the gun and pressed the barrel into the man's groin. Menendez rose to his toes, gasping, breaking out into a stream of rapid Spanish. Laredo

10

ripped the gun's foresight across his clean-shaven cheek.

"Shut up! You and me, we speak only English from now on, savvy? I'm *your commandante*, now."

There were guards hammering at the door, rifle butts thudding against the thick planks.

"Tell 'em to prepare your horse and to bring two more from your stables, one of those Morgans or the Ay-rabs. And I want two mules, one with plenty of food and water. And it better not be poisoned because you're gonna be eating it right along with me. Fact, you'll be eating first. Do it!"

Menendez obeyed with the reeking gun barrel almost in his mouth, his eyes glaring their hatred, but his body oozing the sour sweat of fear. It was strange, but the only prisoner he had ever felt afraid of was this one, this Laredo. From the moment he had arrived Menendez had sensed something different about this Texan. There was a power in him that he knew now — and had sensed then — that no delayed whipping or torture or solitary confinement could ever break.

Now, for the moment anyway, the man had the upper hand.

But, of course, the fool could never hope to get through the Rebano gates alive . . .

Emilio Menendez was completely wrong.

In less than half an hour he was roped to the saddle of his big black Arab and the muzzles of a double-barrelled shot-gun were fastened to the back of his neck with bandages, tied tightly, holding the cold metal hard against his sweat-slippery flesh. The other end of the gun was in Laredo's right hand, which was held in place by rawhide, his finger on the triggers, the hammers cocked.

Even if any fool of a guard shot him, the shot-gun would still explode by the reflex action of his trigger finger and *El Commandante*'s brains would be spread all over the bleak Sonoran landscape.

The Texan rode a hardy little mule, and the extra two horses, both Morgans, and the packmule followed on a long rawhide rope.

There was silence on the walls of the hated prison as Laredo and his hostage rode away. But down in the cells and quarry and the punishment yards, there was singing and shouting and wild yelling.

The prisoners would pay later, of course, but for now they didn't care. Someone had at last beaten the feared *commandante*, killed his most sadistic guards and *El Latigo* as well.

This was indeed a day of celebration — and who cared if tomorrow would bring back Hell? They had lived there for years already and who cared if they survived or not?

Death was at least a form of release from this purgatory on earth.

Meanwhile, Laredo and Menendez rode slowly away, heading for — of all places — the distant Sierra Madre where the Mexicans would be mighty reluctant to follow.

For the Madre was the last hiding place of the Apaches and only a loco fool would deliberately head in there.

★ ★ ★

Emilio Menendez was disappointed — and scared white. Nothing he had depended on to end this nightmare had happened.

He was sure Laredo would cave in under the strain. While he did feed his prisoners tolerably well, he only gave them sufficient food to produce enough high-quality sandstone for the haciendas of far-off Mexico City to keep the administration happy. He did not believe the prison diet he had personally devised would give any prisoner foolish enough to even attempt escape — and none had escaped Rebano before this — enough stamina to get more than a couple of miles.

14

But Laredo showed no sign of weakening. The man slept lightly, dozed in the saddle during the day, making Menendez sweat and his bowels turn to water in case he jerked that shot-gun trigger while dreaming.

He knew the search attempt would be half-hearted. None of his men would care to venture into the Sierra Madre. They had made raids in the past, hitting the *rancherias* with Menendez's blessing and, on several occasions, under his leadership. For the Mexican Government still paid bounty on Apache scalps. One hundred pesos for a young male warrior; fifty pesos for the scalp of a mature woman; and twenty-five for the scalp of an Apache child, male or female.

Some of his men had grown rich by supplementing their meagre pay in this manner. He had himself built up a nice nest-egg. But the Apaches hated the Mexicans and had on several occasions turned the tables on the raiding parties. Now, no one seemed eager to ride far into the mountains chasing scalps, after they found the remains . . .

If they came across a roving band of Apaches, that was fine, but they feared the mountains. And that included Menendez. He knew what would happen to him if ever Apaches caught him alive.

"We must turn west, *señor*," he gasped on the third sweltering morning. They had paused on a ridge to look back, but there was no haze of dust that might have indicated pursuit. "The Apaches are everywhere here . . . "

Laredo nodded. He looked some different to the prisoner who had fled Rebano. He had used Menendez's toilet kit, scissors first, then sweet-smelling shaving soap and finally a honed razor with carved ivory handles and an inlaid silver design.

"Must be worth a lot this," he commented and *El Commandante* agreed, offering it to Laredo as a gift. The Texan had made the Rebano men bring the *commandante*'s cash box

16

from the safe in his office and he had blown the lock off with the Le Mat and found five hundred in gold pesos and another hundred in silver. The paper money was useless to him. The cash was little enough after five years in Rebano.

He had trimmed his hair. It was still long, thick about ears and neck, but that was how he used to wear it all those years ago when he was punching cows on the Chisholm Trail. His skin was sun-blackened and there were two short but deep scars on his face, one from a guard's spur, the other from *El Latigo*'s whip when he had slightly misjudged a stroke, or so he claimed. He now wore peon clothes, the baggy cotton trousers and shirt, a faded red cummerbund in which he had thrust the revolver and a knife. There were antelope leather sandals on his feet and a large sombrero on his head.

He rode the mule because it was better than a horse in this mountain country.

The third night, deep into the Madre, camped under piñon, Laredo roped Menendez to a tree, sitting down so he could strap the shotgun to his hand again when he slept close by.

Next morning, *El Commandante* complained that fire ants had kept him awake all night and Laredo saw the large green-and-black glinting bodies as they scurried about Menendez's feet. Apparently they were down inside his once immaculate half boots.

Laredo removed the boots, saw the angry bites, dozens of them. He traced the ants back to their nest a few feet away. They had come to get the food scraps from his supper and some had apparently detoured by way of Menendez.

Laredo surprised the *commandante* then by unlashing the shot-gun from his neck and placing it with the packs. Then he proceeded to saddle up his mule, strapped the packs on the other mule, but left the three horses on the picket line, Menendez's ornate, silver-inlaid saddle on the ground.

The Mexican, sweat stinging his eyes, watched, puzzled. Then Laredo cut some bark from a tree and scooped up a large section of the fire ants' nest. He dumped it over Menendez's bare feet.

The man's eyes almost popped from their sockets. "No! No, *amigo*! Don't do this, please! I implore you! I give you anything . . . !"

Laredo mounted his mule. "I've got all I want for now, Emilio, old *amigo*. I leave you with the ants. If you can struggle free, fine. Otherwise . . . " He shrugged. "Your screams ought to bring the Apaches. Think I saw one or two up the slope just after daybreak. Hey, consider the ants a gift, eh? From all the poor bastards still in Rebano, and all the others buried on that lousy hill in unmarked graves. Oh, the horses are for the Apaches. They sure love fine horseflesh, whether they're riding it or eating it. *Adios*, Emilio. I hope you find all the men you sent to Hell waiting for you when you finally arrive — which won't be for a long, long time if I know how Apaches work."

He flicked a mocking salute, his sombrero hanging down his back, revealing his pale hair. This way the Apaches would know he was not a Mexican and they wouldn't bother him after leaving them such a fine present.

He could hear Menendez's screams for an hour and then the final one changed in timbre, quavering in total terror and agony . . .

The Apaches had found him.

★ ★ ★

He made his way down out of the Madre and its green timber and flowing streams. He crossed the Rio Margarita and south-west of Chinapos was caught by a rain storm that threatened to wash away the trail from beneath the feet of his plodding mules.

Flash floods turned the arroyos

into muddy, swift-flowing streams and although he crossed two easily enough, the third was rising too fast for him to risk it. He sought out a cutbank well above water level and settled down to wait. Visibility was limited to a few yards, the rain was so heavy.

After about an hour with the muddy water churning up the sides of the arroyo and making him ready himself to leave his shelter, he saw something, off to his left, this side of the muddy torrent. It looked like a downed horse. There was no movement from the animal but he was certain something out there was moving behind it. The rider, maybe, trapped underneath?

He was standing in the rain, enjoying its coolness and the softness as it washed some of the accumulated jail filth from him. He shielded his eyes with his hand for he was hatless, hair plastered to his head by the rain. Yeah — something moved out there.

Taking the shot-gun, he moved up on to the rim and, crouching all the way, he reached a point above the downed animal. He looked over cautiously, wary of the rain-softened edges in case they gave way under his hand.

He had been right. There was a man trapped down there, one leg caught beneath the horse. And he was an Apache.

He had removed his headband and it was wrapped in a crude bandage about his upper left arm. The rain hadn't yet washed all the dried blood away and some of it reached to his wrist. Laredo saw that the horse's rump had had sections of hide and meat cut from it so he guessed the Indian had been here for some days, was eating his dead horse to stay alive.

The horse itself obviously had a broken neck and if it hadn't been raining so heavily he was sure he would have seen the signs where the bank had given way and the animal had toppled back, snapping its neck against the jutting rock on the way down, pinning the Apache before he could get clear. Obviously, he was wounded in the left arm and likely he had been dozing or out of his head with fever when the accident had happened.

As Laredo watched, the man's eyelids opened and he lifted his right hand, holding his stag-handled knife, and brushed strands of hair aside. Two black orbs like the muzzles of cocked six-guns stared up into Laredo's face.

"Is your leg broken?"

The Apache gave a start at being addressed in his own language. But he said nothing.

Laredo climbed down, holding the shot-gun on him, seeing the large hooked nose, the steel-trap mouth and those eyes burning with hate. There was a short scar below one ear.

"Put down your knife and I will try to free you," Laredo said, laying down the shot-gun, well out of the man's reach.

The Indian frowned, looked at the shot-gun and the Le Mat as Laredo laid it beside the weapon. He tensed when the Texan pulled out the big-bladed Bowie knife he had taken from Rebano. "Now lay aside that knife of yours and I'll try to dig under your hoss, OK?"

The Indian watched his every move and only after the fourth request from Laredo, did he put the knife back into his belt sheath.

The Texan dug, stopping frequently, making sure the Indian wasn't about to knife him. Some were so fanatical in their hatred of whites that they would want the pleasure of killing one even if it meant he could not be freed and would die here.

But the Apache merely watched, wincing once or twice when the digging allowed the horse to settle on his trapped leg. It could be broken, but he wasn't going to show this white man whether he was in pain or not.

Laredo kept an eye on the rising water, worked faster when he heard a distant roar way back up the arroyo, likely in one of the narrow canyons

Bladen County Public Library
Elizabethtown, N. C. 28337

up there. The flood was on its way down . . . The dead horse was settling slowly in the disturbed mud, pressing down on the leg. The Texan turned as something pushed against his back. The Apache was thrusting a rock towards him. He nodded, took it and pushed it beneath the carcass. The Indian rolled a second head-sized rock down and Laredo placed this on the other side of the leg.

The roar of the approaching water was making the sodden ground tremble. The Indian propped himself up on one elbow, tried to scoop out some of the mud. His face was impassive but when Laredo saw the gash in the leg where it rested on a sharp rock he wondered how the man could bear it.

He worked faster, stopped digging, grabbed the man beneath the arms and heaved. The Apache grunted and he looked kind of sallow but his leg wouldn't slide free. The Texan began digging again, faster, cutting a finger on his knife blade. He

25
C·1

glanced over the reeking carcass of the horse. Something moved wraith-like up the arroyo. Muddy water and foam splashing above the rim of the narrow gash in the slope.

Then he saw the debris being carried along — a dead tree, bushes, the carcass of an antelope or bighorn sheep, and he knew there was a solid wall of water smashing towards them and it would rise above where they now were.

The mules had already moved up and away by instinct. He grabbed the Indian again. "This is gonna hurt, chief, and if you don't come free I'm gonna have to leave you and make a run for it."

The Apache said nothing but Laredo felt the man tense and then he placed his right foot against the horse and began to push as Laredo pulled. That sharp rock embedded in his calf ripped at the flesh and the mud clung until it began to make sucking sounds that Laredo could hear above the thunder of the floodwaters.

Suddenly, he sprawled flat on his back and the Indian was limp in his hands. He dug in with the sandals and thrust backwards up the slope. After the initial heave, he found more leverage and he grunted and panted and slipped and strained, heaving the Apache up the slope away from the chocolate-coloured wall of water-borne debris surging into the arroyo. He heaved the inert man up on to a flat spot, slid back desperately, snatching the shot-gun and pistol, falling and clawing at the mud, on his knees, waddling up like a duck as the water hit the bend with a tremendous thud that shook the ground and spurted debris and mud and water fifteen feet into the air. He kept straining for the flat land where he had dumped the Indian, felt water tugging at his feet, halfway up his calf, to his knees, his legs washed sideways . . .

Then it was past and bearing away the carcass of the dead horse and he sprawled beside the Indian, gasping for breath.

After a while he sat up, saw the Apache was still unconscious and figured that would be the best time to work on that mangled leg, so he started first aid by working out the rock, seeing the broken bits embedded in the raw flesh.

The wound had to be cleaned, packed with rags, bandaged, and then the bullet had to be removed from the man's upper arm. The water had washed away the dirty headband and he saw the wound was festering, purple and swollen with infection. He knew there were plenty of white men — Mexicans, too — who would not thank him for what he was about to do.

No one living along the border would. The maxim they lived by in that country was that 'The only good Apache is a dead Apache'.

He worked over the Indian, cleansing the leg wound and bandaging it, then searched for enough dry wood to build a small fire under a shelter of rocks so he could cauterize the arm wound after he had dug out the bullet.

He had no idea who the Apache was.

It probably wouldn't have made any difference. He had suffered so much these past five years, witnessed so much true misery, that he couldn't abide it in *any* human being, white, black, red or any other colour.

Except Emilio Menendez: but he was special, that one.

And as for this Apache who writhed and groaned under Laredo's knife as he probed for the bullet, well, he would live.

For better or for worse.

2

IT was five weeks before he rode back to the Mogollon Rim.

No one would have recognized the emaciated, hollow-eyed prisoner who had done the impossible and escaped from Rebano jail, then made it safely back to the United States.

Laredo was a mite more stooped than when he had last ridden through this country, but he still topped the six feet mark by a couple of inches. He had put some meat back on his bones during the past month or so under the care of a sawbones named Cullen, an old friend from the war, in the medic's cool adobe house on the outskirts of the wide, grey dust bowl surrounding Bisbee, Arizona.

He was wearing a cowboy's outfit now, all new a month ago, purchased with the gold he had taken from

Menendez's safe. Old habits die hard and he had bought himself a fringed, pull-over buckskin shirt, worn outside his sand-coloured drill trousers and a similar coloured flat-crowned, wide-brimmed hat. This attempt at making himself as invisible as possible against the landscape came from his time scouting for the army. He hadn't fought his war in all the now famous battlefields. He had never been at Bull Run, First or Second, nor at Gettysburg or Shiloh. He had been baptized by fire in the hell of Fredericksburg and then he had been sent West to help deal with the Indian problem. Many of the tribes, especially the Comanches, Kiowa and Apaches, were taking advantage of the Civil War's depletion of troops out West and had busted out of reservations and happily returned to the warpath, raiding and killing settlers.

It was while in pursuit of one of these bands of Apaches that he had first seen his land, a full section of lush green, treed and watered land on the Mogollon Rim.

Now he could hardly wait to get back up there.

He had bought himself a new gun rig, a Smith and Wesson breaktop pistol that took the new copper ·44 rimfire cartridges. He also bought a '66 Model Winchester, foregoing the convenience of a saddle carbine for the extra range and greater accuracy of a full-size rifle.

He forked a roan gelding now that had a nick out of the tip of the left ear, obviously made by a bullet in the past. A line-backed dun toted his packs.

Laredo came in through the Tonto basin, noting the ranches and towns that had expanded during his absence. He stopped in Wildman Creek to rest his mounts and himself before the long climb out and up to the Rim.

It had been a mighty long journey from Rebano, and it hadn't been an easy one. After he had crossed the San Miguel River bandits had set upon him but he had faced them with such fury, killing six of their number and wounding the other three that they had given up chasing him just short of the border. Which was just as well, because he had used up all his ammunition.

Yeah, luck had ridden with him all the way. And about time. He was due for a change for the better.

So he was really looking forward to getting back to his own land up on the Rim where likely Barr and Drew had turned the spread into a profitable business. Not that it mattered.

It would just be so good to be back with his pards and riding his own land again, green and lush and, hopefully, dotted with cattle bearing his own brand: a simple back-to-back Double L — Laredo's Land.

It was the first land he had ever owned and as far as he was concerned it would be the last, for he didn't want to live anywhere else. The valley he had first seen, with its stream, two small waterfalls, patches of gramma grass and clumps of timber, had struck him like a physical blow right in the middle of his chest. Something had happened to him: he was far from being a romantic, but Laredo felt that day that this place was where he *belonged*, where his heart wanted to be.

So he had filed on a full section, proved-up by the deadline and just as he was making big plans for the future — and wondering how the hell he was going to carry them out — Drew and Barr had shown up. Couldn't have arrived at a better time and soon the old wartime partnership was functioning full-swing.

Riding into Wildman Creek, aware of the stares of folk on the street, he saw this was a raw place, the buildings mostly unpainted and not yet weathered to the usual grey. He saw some placer mining just outside the town and the way it nestled back under the Tonto Rim gave it a picturesque look. He hauled suddenly as a freight wagon — Star Freight Line — cut across his bows and almost hit the roan's swinging head.

"Watch your driving, *amigo*!" he called curtly.

The driver, a big man with black stubble fringing a lantern jaw and an arrogant look to his mouth, spat in Laredo's direction, kept moving, but deliberately swung the wagon in close, forcing Laredo to wrench the roan aside again.

The man glared back, his dark eyes challenging. Laredo held the stare, blank-faced, sat there until the man ran his wagon into a freight yard on the other side of the street.

Damn. Normally, he would have that ranny on the ground by now, a boot across his neck, extracting an apology, but he felt too good about going home and didn't want trouble. The hell with him, anyway. Some local bully by the look of him.

He turned his horses into a livery, rubbed them down himself and arranged with the hostler for feeding and stalling overnight. The man directed him to

The Kelly House, a kind of saloon with rooming-house attached.

"Good grub, tolerably clean sheets," the hostler told him, then winked. "Could be if you happen to go into the wrong room, you might find an accommodatin' lady, if you're so inclined."

Laredo smiled faintly. "I'll remember that."

He booked a room, washed-up and headed for the saloon. The whiskey was terrible, nearly tore out his throat, and the meal he ordered brought to a rear table where he took his foaming beer, was barely adequate. But, after the muck he had eaten in Rebano, day after day, year after year, it was a royal feast. Trouble was, Doc Cullen's wife had spoiled him with her marvellous stews and roasts and baked apple pies.

He finished the meal with a slice of soggy peach pie and another beer. The room was large, the roof beams exposed, and the stairs to the rooms above where the soiled doves carried

36

out their business were little better than a glorified ladder. There were several crude tables scattered about the dirt floor where men sat drinking or dreaming, dull-eyed, or playing cards. Others, some in miner's clothes, mud all over their trousers and boots, others in range outfits, lounged at the bar. This was only a couple of planks resting across empty beer kegs and the barkeep was likely the toughest-looking customer Laredo had ever seen.

He was rolling himself a smoke, one leg propped up on a vacant chair, when a shadow fell across him and a rough voice said, "Well, what we got here? Only the champeen streethog of the Muggyown!"

It was the freighter, of course, and Laredo could smell the whiskey on his breath from where he sat. He emanated other, even less pleasant odours, too, but nothing that affected Laredo much, not after five years in Rebano.

The man's face was rugged, carried a few scars and these, together with the nose that listed to port, labelled him as a brawler. Laredo figured he was about his own age, mid-thirties, and he looked hard as a tree as he leaned his big, calloused knuckles on the edge of the table.

"Now you're hoggin' my favourite table, mister."

Laredo put his cigarette between his lips, snapped a vesta into flame. Before he could dip the end of the cigarette into it, the freighter reached across and pinched it out. He grinned down at Laredo.

"I only allow my friends to smoke at my table."

Laredo sighed, saw where this was inevitably leading. He stood up slowly, faced the freighter, saw the others in the bar watching, grinning, nudging one another, waiting for the fun to start. He looked levelly into the big man's eyes.

"Suppose I moved to the table yonder?"

The freighter's grin widened. "Why,

that's reserved for my friends, mister."

Laredo nodded. "Thought it'd be something like that. That one over there?"

The freighter shook his head, still grinning. "Fact is, mister, there ain't anywheres in this room where you could sit that won't crowd me."

"Yeah, that's what I figured. I guess it'd be OK if I went up to my own room next door?"

"Well, I dunno about that — I just ain't took to you at all. Might be best if you moved on clear outa town. There's plenty good campin' spots along the crick."

Laredo pursed his lips. "I don't think so. I'd be just as likely to choose a spot that you fancied."

The freighter chuckled. "You know, you just might at that!" He turned to his grinning audience. "This is one smart feller we got here."

"Seems to me, no matter what I do, I'm gonna end up tanglin' with you."

"Man, you are so right there!"

"OK." Laredo's right hand came up in a blur and the Smith and Wesson crashed across the side of the freighter's head, knocking him halfway across the room. He went down, taking two sets of tables and chairs with him. He began to push upright, pure fighting instinct driving him, for his eyes were already out of focus, and Laredo walked across, whipped the gun barrel across his head again and laid the man out on the dirt floor.

Holding the six-gun casually, he looked around at the suddenly sober-faced men in the room. "Anyone want to take up the argument on his behalf?"

No one did, but the barkeep was frozen, one shoulder lowered as he grasped something slung beneath the bar. Laredo waved his gun at the man.

"Straighten up, *amigo*. Now."

The man did so, slowly, hard-faced, wary.

"I was you, Texan, I wouldn't hang

around this here town for long." He gestured to the gun-whipped man. "Dancey hits the booze at the end of a run and he's always poison-mean with a hangover. After what you done to him . . . " He let it hang.

"I'll be moving up to the Mogollon Rim come daylight. Tell Dancey if I see him again, he better be ready for a damn hard fight. Guns or fists, makes no nevermind to me. He can choose."

The barkeep pursed his lips. "I just don't think you're quite that tough, Texan."

"A lot of men have made the same mistake. Why not you? Or Dancey . . . ?"

The 'keep nodded. "I'll let him sleep it off in the storeroom. Might kinda lock the door — accidental like."

Laredo nodded his thanks, left some money on the table and went out. He didn't holster the gun until he was back in his room next door to the saloon.

* * *

The sun hadn't touched Cuchillo Creek when Laredo crossed it the next morning.

The shadows were dark and cool and birds were still awakening in the willows and sycamores and something was making a splash in a clump of cat's-tails to his left. He liked the cool after all the heat he had endured these past five years and slowed the horse on the eastern bank, folding his hands on the saddle horn, watching the dun graze lazily.

Something whipped air past his left ear and an instant later he heard the crack of a rifle and he dived out of the saddle. His Winchester was too long to slide easily out of the scabbard as he left leather, so he grabbed the sheath itself and allowed his falling weight to snap the rawhide tie thongs that held it in place. Once he hit the bank, he rolled, grasping the rifle stock and making a flinging motion

42

that freed it of the scabbard which sailed away six feet or more. Then he squirmed in behind the grass the line-backed dun had been chewing and two more bullets kicked sand against his shoulder. The lever worked smoothly and the brass-bound butt fitted snugly into his shoulder as he sighted along the flat top of the octagonal barrel, the foresight searching for his attacker.

He saw the cloud of gunsmoke, heard the thud of the rifle again and picked it out as being an old Spencer, likely ·52 calibre as that was the most popular, but it sounded heavy enough with all these trees around to be possibly ·56 calibre. Either way, the bushwhacker had him pinned.

The big ball spewed sand and grass into his face and he slid back, boots trailing in the water. He lunged up and over sideways, splashing into the water and wriggling under a cutbank as the rifle boomed three times, swiftly, the lead chewing away at the edge of the bank.

Laredo rolled out from under, came up on to his knees, rifle at his shoulder, working lever and trigger as he raked the killer's shelter with five shots that seemed to blend into a single prolonged roar. He heard a man curse, glimpsed a body rearing back and triggered again. The man's hat spun away and then he dropped from sight.

The Texan came up out of the water and leapt on to the bank, running in zigzag fashion towards the trees. Again he glimpsed his quarry running through the bushes, doubled over. The Texan snapped a shot at him and the man veered away, dropped out of sight. Laredo slowed, crouched under a willow, waiting for the echoes of gunfire to die away so he could hear any sounds the killer might make while trying to creep up on him.

But the only sounds he eventually heard were the rapid-fire beats of racing hoofs. He ran out and forward, still wary in case the man had only sent his horse running off to make Laredo

44

think he was quitting.

But it was the killer, all right. Laredo sent him on his way over the crest of a rise with two hammering shots, then slowly walked back to his horses where he reloaded thoughtfully.

Not at any time had he seen the bushwhacker clearly, but he had the impression it had been Dancey.

He rode cautiously after that, fording Carrizo Creek and swimming his horses across Cibecue. He headed out along the White Mountain Trail to the Rim and once up there, a thousand feet above the Tonto Basin, he paused to take his look at one of the most beautiful valleys in all of the USA. He drank in the lushness and the greens, the reds and greys of canyons, the silver flashes of waterfalls, the dark moving dots of animals, deer, antelope, a few buffalo, some mustangs in bunches. Yeah, this was his country, and he was mighty glad to be back.

Well, no time to be dreaming when he was this close. Might as well ride on in and be that one step closer. Then, come morning, he could ride out to his land. He sure hoped Barr and Drew were still around. They had been drifters and although he had taken them into partnership — sealed with a grin and a nod, not even a handshake, sure nothing in writing — he had wondered then just how long it would be before they tired of ranch life and drifted on.

Well, he hoped they were still there. If not, his land would be and he was looking forward to clearing it all over again and rebuilding it to the stage he had reached before that fateful run down into Mexico.

* * *

Five years ago, the town of Sinola had been little more than a few scattered tents and only two buildings, the saloon and Murphy's General Store. Now it was a cluster of clapboard falsefronts all along Main, businesses ranging from a livery through draperies, a drug store and even a bakery and, yes, a large freight yard at the south end. Even from the opposite end of Main he could see the big yellow star painted above the gate. Frame houses dotted the slopes around the business centre and he counted three saloons now and another general store almost opposite Murphy's with the name Cheetam's Emporium painted in a crude arc across the otherwise raw wood falsefront.

He didn't expect to find anyone in town that he knew, except maybe Murphy, or even La Salle from the saloon, although he hadn't seemed the kind to stay long in one place. The hostler was neither friendly nor hostile, answered questions courteously enough, but added nothing. He asked for payment in advance and Laredo flicked him a silver dollar and, shouldering warbag and rifle went to the saloon that had belonged to La Salle. It had sure changed, lined inside, painted garishly, a small stage across one end where an over-painted, overweight woman was singing "Poor Granny Lee" — out of tune — and there were faro and blackjack layouts as well as house gamblers running card games, mostly draw poker.

Thing was, the place was crowded so he figured the area must be prosperous, which pleased him. The barkeeps were all strangers, hassled off their feet and sweating, no time to do more than ask for a man's order and fill it as quickly as possible.

"La Salle still own this place?" the Texan asked the apron who brought his beer.

The man, balding, pigeon-chested, frowned. "Never heard of no La Salle. I been here two years an' it's always been managed by Will Benedict."

As he started to turn away, Laredo said mildly, "I asked about the owner, not the manager."

The man scowled, was about to make a terse remark but something in the Texan's sun-blackened, scarred face made him clear his throat and he said, "Hear it's some local rancher owns it."

Laredo grabbed the man's arm this time and the barkeep's eyes flared and he reached for a billy. The Texan stared coldly into his eyes and said quietly, "Don't do that, friend. You've been here two years and you've *heard* the place is owned by a local rancher."

The 'keep swallowed. "Listen, I got no time . . . "

"He's right. This is a busy night," said a voice behind Laredo and he turned to see a man in flowered vest and string tie with wavy black hair above a handsome but somehow weak face smiling at him. The smile was pleasant enough but it stopped short of his cool, appraising eyes. "You run along, Mike."

The 'keep pulled free and hurried away and the man said, "I'm Will Benedict. Anything I can do for you?"

Laredo hesitated, shook his head, then said, lifting his beer, "Just asked if

La Salle still owned this place but your man started to give me the run around. Guess I'm just tired and a little edgy. Hadn't noticed till he started double-talking me."

"Well, La Salle quit about three years back. Killed in a gunfight. With the present owner, matter of fact."

"Local rancher according to Mike."

Benedict smiled faintly. "Uh-huh. He's got a good few business interests in Sinola. The saloon is only one of them." Laredo waited and Benedict added, "Freight line, cathouse down Powder Lane, partners with Cheetham in a general store, and a couple other things."

"He got a name?"

"Now, friend, I was just wondering the same thing about you."

"They call me Laredo."

Benedict was in the act of lighting a cheroot when the Texan spoke and his hand paused an inch short of the end. Then he touched the flame to the cheroot and shook out the match and ground it under his boot before setting his gaze on Laredo's face again.

"Just 'Laredo'"?"

"That's what I answer to."

"You're from there?"

"Not lately, but originally. Mean anything to you?"

Benedict shook his head swiftly. "No, no — I've heard the name, of course, applied to other men . . ."

"You were gonna tell me who this rich *hombre* is who owns this place and half the town."

"Well, no, friend, I wasn't, actually — I was wondering why your interest?"

Laredo sighed. "It started out casual. I knew La Salle, not well, but I knew him five, six years back, and I wondered if he was still around. Your barkeep made a mystery out of it — and I don't like mysteries."

Benedict stared down at his cheroot end. "Tough for you."

Laredo smiled crookedly. "And, Benedict, I ain't really all that interested. But I've got my own spread outside of town and I like to know the names of the local business folk I'll be dealing with."

The saloon man frowned. "I don't recall you."

"Been away for about five years, but I'm back now. My spread's the Double L, out on the rim by Diamond Butte."

Benedict frowned deeply, stared hard, his cheroot halfway to his mouth. Laredo tensed, watched the man in silence for a long minute, and then Benedict said, "I don't think so, friend."

The tension in Laredo began to knot his belly. "You don't?"

"No — there's no Double L spread around here. Biggest ranch in the territory is out Diamond Butte way, but that's the Star Bar."

"Star? Same man who runs Star Freight?"

Benedict hesitated, nodded. "Mr Barr Gannon."

Laredo's face showed nothing but his

knuckles whitened around the handle of the beer mug.

Barr Gannon . . .

"He got a partner named Drew?" he asked, annoyed that his voice sounded so raspy.

Benedict shook his head slowly. "He don't have no pardners at all."

"That's all you know," Laredo said grimly. "You got rooms to let in this place?"

Benedict nodded, not taking his eyes off the big Texan, sensing something in this man that made him break out in a cold sweat. "Sure, I got a room you can have for the night. Grab your warbag and follow me."

It was a good room, overlooking Main, with a balcony and a good strong lock on the door. Laredo washed-up and turned in, too tired to eat.

But he slept with his hand on his six-gun under his pillow and the rifle with a cartridge in the chamber on the chair beside the bed.

Something had gone out of his homecoming since he had spoken with Will Benedict.

★ ★ ★

"Whatever this is it better be damn good, Will, draggin' me outa bed like this."

Barr Gannon was tall and wide-shouldered, but his hips were lean and his legs extra long so that he had an all-over rangy appearance. His face was narrow, hawk-like, the eyes piercing, his hair short and light brown.

Benedict, sweating from his fast ride from town, accepted the offer of whiskey and then blurted out, "Feller calling himself Laredo just hit town. Hinted he was your pardner. Asked about Drew."

Gannon went very still, remained silent for so long that Benedict shifted restlessly. Then he looked up and spoke so quietly that Benedict wasn't sure just what he said.

54

"Couldn't be."

"I never met the man, Mr Gannon, but I recollect you talking about him once or twice."

Gannon's eyes narrowed. "You got a damn good memory, ain't you, Benedict?"

The saloon man smiled, a mite tightly. "Never know when what you remember could do you some good."

Gannon's face looked murderous and it was a long minute before he was back in complete control.

"Ward back yet?"

"He came in just after sundown, I believe."

"Go back and tell him to cut the booze and get back here. I want him here tonight — savvy?"

Benedict nodded. "I'll tell him, Mr Gannon . . . er, is there anything else?"

Gannon's cold stare touched the saloon man's. "No," he said flatly and Benedict looked some disappointed but didn't push it.

He'd remember he'd done Gannon

this favour. He'd remember — when it would be to his advantage. As the rancher said, he had a mighty good memory . . . whether it was aided by a tip or not.

3

THE country had changed.

No, not the country, it was still as he recollected, plenty of trees and streams and good grass, rugged bare spines of rock splitting the land right to the Rim itself in places, huge, expansive vistas over the basin and beyond.

But there were ranches out here now. Others who had proved-up as he had, Laredo supposed. Some small, some medium-sized, all with good range and there were many kinds of cattle at graze: longhorns, Herefords, some Jerseys on one place that had a lot of crops planted — which might make it more of a farm than a ranch. Well, he was strictly cattle and horses himself but this land had room for all. He wouldn't care much to live shoulder to shoulder with a nester, but he guessed he could put up with it if he had to.

But, swinging in along the Three Peaks Trail that eventually led to Diamond Butte, he spotted cattle on range that must sweep back almost to touch his own. There was a curl of smoke way back beyond a stand of timber where he figured there was a ranch house. He could see some corrals where a couple of men were busy busting half-tamed mustangs to the saddle, and other riders going about their range chores.

It intrigued him, for this ranch would be his neighbour. So he dismounted from the roan amongst some boulders and took out the old battered field glasses that had come with the second-hand saddle-bags he had bought. They had seen plenty of action in the war, were stamped 'US', which made them Yankee in origin. The lenses had seen better days but they were good enough.

He focused on that stand of timber and the magnification allowed him to see between the trees and pick out the vague shape of a sprawling log-built house with a steep shingle roof: like someone was expecting mighty cold winters and hoped to shed the snow in this way. Well, they were right about the cold: winters on the Rim reminded him of the Dakotas in January.

He glimpsed the other ranch buildings and corrals, movement of animals and men. This was a pretty big place, all right, larger than his Double L, unless Barr and Drew had added to the simple log cabin he had built.

The snick of a gun hammer behind him froze Laredo as he was sweeping the glasses back towards the bronco busters. He started to turn his head but a voice snapped, "Don't! Don't move a finger unless I tell you to!"

It was a girl's voice and there was no trace of fear or uncertainty in it. He almost started to roll on to his side so he could get a look at her but then felt the rifle barrel rammed hard against his spine.

"What're you doing here?" The rifle

59

prodded, hurrying his answer.

"Looking."

The rifle muzzle prodded again and it hurt. He gritted his teeth. "Don't get smart with me! What're you up to?"

He sighed, still facing away from her. "I was on my way to Diamond Butte when I noticed the smoke. I didn't know there was a ranch here, so I decided to take a look."

"Diamond Butte? You're going to Star Bar?"

"If that's what it's called now."

"It's always been called that. You're one of Gannon's men?"

"Not one of his men, no."

"You're going to work at Star Bar?"

"I reckon so."

"Then you're one of Gannon's men, damn you!" She prodded hard with the rifle muzzle and he decided he'd had enough, even as she said, "You carry your gun like a gunfighter . . . "

Then he twisted, fast and hard, the hand holding the field glasses smashing against the rifle barrel, knocking it almost out of the girl's hands. But he swung his legs, too, swept hers out from under her, and she gave a small cry as she stumbled, then sat down in the dust.

By then he had the rifle and was on one knee looking down at her.

She was average size, he figured, showing female curves even under the disarrayed calfskin vest over a checked blouse. She wore a divided buckskin riding skirt, tooled half-boots, and gloves. When he finally looked at her face he saw that it was white and angry right now, full lips compressed beneath a pert nose, bright blue eyes glaring icily at him. Her hat hung askew, caught at her throat by the thong, and lots of taffy-coloured hair framed her face, somewhat raggedly at this moment.

"Give me back my Winchester!"

It was a saddle carbine and Laredo worked the lever swiftly, ejecting five shells on to the ground. Leaving the action open, he handed her the gun butt first.

"You aim to ride around holding up strangers, miss, you'd do well to keep your magazine full."

She was angry enough to spit, he figured, and she held the gun so tightly he thought she might even bend the barrel.

"You get off my land!"

He arched his eyebows. "Your land? I thought this was the Three Peaks Trail?"

"Well, it is — but my land starts just down there."

He grinned. "Then I ain't trespassing. What spread is that?"

"Three Peaks, if it's any of your business. It's my father's place. I help him run it."

"And you are . . . ?"

"Teresa Backmann." He saw the extra flush as new anger spread through her because she had answered without thinking. "Damn you, you were spying?"

He shook his head once. "Nope. Just curious."

"Who are you?"

"They call me Laredo."

"Yes, I picked up the Texas accent." She sounded as if she didn't think too much of Texans. "You won't be the first Texas gunslinger Barr Gannon has hired."

"Well, I dunno that he's gonna hire me."

"But you hope he will! You're one of the drifters who've heard about his generous pay, I suppose, and rode up here on the off-chance that he might put you on his payroll."

"Well, no, it's not exactly like that . . . "

She couldn't contain herself any longer and stamped her foot, raising a small puff of dust. "I don't care a damn how it is! You get away from Three Peaks, you hear? Or I'll signal some of my men and you'll wish you'd done as I asked then, I can tell you."

He nodded. "You sure are steamed-up. But I'll be moving right along." He walked to his roan and by the time he had swung into the saddle, she had scooped up two or three of the ejected cartridges and was pushing them through the loading gate. He grinned again, shook his head hard, and tossed off a brief salute, turning the roan, with the packhorse following lazily.

"If I ever see you near my place again, I'll shoot first and talk afterwards!"

"I have no doubt of that, Miss Backmann!" he said maddeningly and rode on along the trail, stuffing the field glasses back into a saddle-bag.

He did not look back and realized he hadn't even seen what kind of horse she was riding. Must have ground-hitched it back amongst the larger boulders.

Only twenty minutes' slow ride later, he came to the Star Bar gate.

It surprised him as he rounded the butte and saw the big lodgepole arched gateway straddling the trail. There were three men with rifle butts resting on their thighs, waiting.

They looked as if they were waiting for him.

He heeled the roan slowly forward, right hand resting on his thigh, close to his Smith and Wesson, but riding easy just the same.

"Far enough." The man who spoke seemed familiar and it was a moment before Laredo realized it was Dancey, the man he had tangled with in Wildman Creek. But the man was clean-shaven now, except for a popular-style frontier moustache and trimmed sideburns, and he wore decent and clean range clothes.

But he sure didn't look any friendlier and, actually, without the beard, the true ruggedness of his face was plain to see.

Laredo stopped ten feet from the riders who had brought their guns down to menace him when he hadn't hauled rein as soon as Dancey had spoken.

He noticed that Dancey held a Spencer carbine and he smiled crookedly, indicating the gun.

"You're a pretty good shot with that. Almost nailed me down at the old high-side Cuchillo Creek crossing."

Dancey scowled and spat by way of reply. The others were tough-looking hardcases, but it was plain they were awaiting orders from Dancey.

"Gannon around?"

"*Mister* Gannon. He ain't seein' anyone right now."

"He'll see me. I'm his pardner in the Double L or Star Bar or whatever it's called now."

Dancey shook his head. "No you ain't, mister. You ain't no one's pardner in this spread."

Laredo's face was hard now and Dancey grinned, enjoying the Texan's rising anger. "Why don't we go ask him?"

Dancey pursed his lips, gave it a long minute's stare, then shrugged his shoulders. "Why not? Hi-spade, get his guns."

One of the riders, a medium tall

man with a thick waistline, started to heel his mount forward, but froze when the Smith and Wesson came up to cover him.

"No one takes my weapons."

"Orders," Dancey told him curtly. "An' you got four guns pointed at you, feller."

Laredo tilted his pistol barrel in Dancey's direction. "You're first, Dancey. And I guarantee I'll get all the others before I go down. You want to see if I'm that good, then go ahead and push it."

Silence. Heat waves shimmered. Insects hummed. A cow bellowed in the distance. Horses' tails swished. Sweat popped out on Dancey's battered face. Finally, he swallowed and the sound was clearly audible to everyone there.

"All right. But they stay in leather."

"They do — if yours do."

Dancey waited and his face told Laredo the man was swearing a blue streak in his head. Finally he nodded, lowered his rifle hammer, slid the heavy

Spencer into the saddle sheath. The others still hesitated and he snapped at them to sheath their guns — *now*!

They obeyed and they waited and Laredo smiled. "I guess I'll wait till I reach the house to holster mine." Dancey swore aloud this time, jerked his head for one of the riders, a redhead with a thin smudge of pale stubble, to open the gate.

Laredo followed them slowly up the trail.

It should have been familiar and parts of it were but this trail cut away from the old one and angled across the face of a slope he had once planned to use as part of his home pasture. There were several cows dotted across it, but he saw that there were fences down there indicating the borders of a pasture three times as large as he had ever envisaged.

Many more cows dotted this fenced area and the grass was lush and belly-deep. He saw the house after they rounded a bend and he hauled rein in surprise. The old cabin he and Barr and Drew had used was now dwarfed by a sprawling log and riverstone house with shingle roofs and gables and two stone chimneys. There were vegetable gardens off to one side and disappearing around to the rear. The barn was larger than his old cabin which seemed to have been incorporated into the stables, and there was a network of pole corrals that looked like stockyards at a railhead. The bunkhouse was clapboard, long and narrow, with its own stone fireplace at one end.

The whole place had a mighty prosperous look to it and Laredo felt admiration for Barr Gannon: the man had sure worked his butt off to build Double L into this big a spread. No wonder he had called it Star Bar: it deserved a better name than the mundane one he had thought up on the spur of the moment.

Mind, he still thought of it, at this

stage, as Laredo's Land.

There was a long shady veranda running clear across the front of the house and now he saw movement there in the cool dimness. A man, hatless, dressed in denim shirt and trousers, gun belt slanting across his hard belly, a glass of something in one hand. The man lifted a hand to shade his eyes against the glare and Laredo smiled crookedly.

That was one of Barr's characteristic gestures and although the man was much better groomed than Laredo had ever seen him, he knew it *was* Barr Gannon and no mistake.

Gannon came to the top of the short set of steps and sipped from the glass — it looked like lemonade — as the group walked their mounts into the yard and dismounted. All except Laredo. He sat his roan, still gripping his Smith and Wesson, but unaware that he was doing so.

Dancey walked across, obviously to report to Gannon, while the three hardcases stood near the steps, thumbs hooked into cartridge belts, trying to look tough. They didn't have to work very hard at it.

Gannon flicked his gaze to Laredo and the Texan saw he was clean-shaven, his hair trimmed and even parted neatly on the right. He looked like he had just walked out of a barber's shop and Laredo thought he even smelled a whiff of bay rum.

Dancey was still talking when Gannon stepped past him, smiling up at Laredo, leaving the glass on the top of the railings. He shook his head slowly and thrust up his right hand which Laredo gripped after quickly holstering his pistol.

"Well, tuck me under a grizzly's armpit! It damn well is you, Laredo!"

"In the flesh!" The Texan felt his own face stiffening from the unaccustomed wide grin and he swung down from the saddle with a grunt. He faced Gannon from only a couple of feet away and the rancher's big hands gripped his shoulders. He shook the Texan briefly.

"By God, I thought you were dead! They told me you were — killed by *bandidos* in Sonora."

"It was *Federales*, not bandits. And they didn't kill me, only wounded me. Unfortunately, I shot a couple of them and that earned me a ten-year sentence in Rebano."

Gannon stiffened and even Dancey had a look of respect on his face now. The trio of hardcases murmured amongst themselves.

"You — you goin' to tell me you — escaped? From *Rebano*, for Chrissakes . . . ?"

Laredo nodded. "Spur of the moment. Things just fell together for me. I was mighty lucky."

"Judas, man, you can say that again. Well, come on in to the house. I gotta admit when I heard someone named Laredo was in town an' comin' to see me, I figured it had to be some lousy imposter. Couldn't figure what he'd be after but — come on! Let's get this talked-out over a drink. Or two — or three . . . "

Laredo held back and Gannon frowned. "Somethin' wrong, *amigo*?"

"Where's Drew?"

Gannon stared back, holding the cool level gaze. "Drew's dead. And I *know* that for certain sure."

"What happened?"

"Hell, let's get this talked-out inside, Laredo."

"We'll talk. After you tell me what happened to Drew."

Gannon flicked his eyes to Dancey and said quietly, "Bring the decanter and a couple of glasses out here, Ward, will you?"

Dancey moved away along the veranda without a word and Gannon turned back to Laredo, unsmiling, and maybe just a mite puzzled.

"Drew was killed by Apaches. He was hauling one of my freight wagons when it happened. Bunch of them red bastards hit the wagon and killed everyone there — except Ward, but they thought he was dead otherwise they'd have finished him — and not too quickly."

"Drew died quickly then?"

Gannon hesitated. "I — I don't think so. He was still alive when they took him off."

Laredo looked past Gannon as Dancey appeared with the decanter of whiskey and two glasses, all of which he set on the rails. He frowned and straightened warily when he saw the look on Laredo's face.

"You let the Apaches take Drew while he was still alive?"

Dancey frowned, glanced at Gannon who was now pouring two whiskeys, then ran a tongue around the inside of his bottom lip. "I wasn't in no condition to help him. They'd took my gun. I was bleedin' . . ."

"And you were yellow," cut in Laredo, bringing Gannon's head up with a snap.

"Now, wait up, Laredo," the rancher

said. "You can't blame Ward. They'd've killed him, too, if he'd tried anythin'."

Laredo's eyes drilled into the tight-lipped freighter. "I'd've tried something. If not then, I'd've followed and tried to put Drew out of his misery."

"You'd've done spit!" Dancey snapped, coming down the steps to face the Texan. "I wasn't gonna stick my neck out for that damn hillbilly. Anyways . . . "

Laredo swung, his fist coming up from beside his holster, the knuckles cracking against Dancey's jaw and knocking the man back into the veranda railings. An upright split and Laredo stepped in, sank a fist into Dancey's midriff and as the man's legs folded, the Texan kicked him in the belly. Dancey went down groaning and gagging and Gannon quickly pushed himself between Laredo and the trio of hardcases as they started forward.

"That's enough! Get back, you three — there'll be no more brawlin' in my yard!" His eyes blazed at the Texan.

"You sure ain't got any better rein on that temper of yours, Laredo!"

The Texan faced Gannon, hard-faced. "Drew was your pard, too."

Gannon sighed. "Hell, you don't need to remind me! Ward's a good man. If he says there was nothin' to be done, OK, then I'll take his word for it. Christ, man, he's lucky to be alive himself."

Laredo looked down coldly on the writhing, semi-conscious man. "Yeah," he said flatly, turned as Gannon touched his arm.

"Come on, have a drink and calm down." The rancher handed him a glass of whiskey and Laredo took it, stared into it for a long moment, then lifted the glass, smiled crookedly, gaze steady, steely.

"To Star Bar — and our partnership."

Gannon stiffened and did not raise his glass. "Laredo — I dunno about any partnership."

Laredo went very still, eyes narrowing. "You don't?" he asked quietly. "You don't recollect the three of us — you, me, Drew — standing outside the door of my log cabin, that one yonder, in the evening light with our first bunch of mustangs crowding the corrals, awaiting breaking, and we all three talked it out and drank some lousy Apache *tizwin* Drew had picked up someplace, and we said we'd be partners in the Double L. We'd break them mustangs and sell 'em down in Mexico where Maximilian was supposed to be paying forty bucks a head for good hosses? Then we'd sink that money into cattle after we'd popped the brush all over the Rim and the basin for mavericks? We were gonna be rich in two, three years, Barr. You, Drew — and me." He moved a step closer. "Now you look me square in the eye and tell me you don't recollect that evening."

Gannon's jaws were working, ridges of muscles rippling under the tanned, healthy skin. His eyes weren't friendly, nor were they bleak — they were totally indifferent and Laredo felt a chill grip

77

his belly. He had seen that look on Gannon's face before, just before they went into action with bayonets fixed and Yankees stretching from hell to breakfast . . .

"I remember, Laredo," he said finally and the Texan began to relax. "I likely recollect better than you. But it don't make no difference. You ain't my pardner. This is my spread now."

Laredo couldn't speak right away. He had a queer, unreal feeling, that he wasn't really here, that he was standing on the edge of someone else's nightmare: this couldn't be happening to him. *Couldn't* be . . .

"I homesteaded this land, Barr. Proved-up, got the deeds. This is my land. You might have thrown-up some fancy buildings and you're running your herds on it, but it is my land."

Gannon scrubbed a hand around his jaw, glancing down as Dancey hauled himself on to the steps and sat there, both hands rammed down into his groin, rocking slowly. The hardcases stood tensed and ready to move on Gannon's signal.

"Laredo, you have to savvy somethin', somethin' that everythin' hinges on — I was told you were *dead*. The word was official. The Land Agency sold your land to me seein' as you had no kin and we was pardners."

"Oh, the partnership still counted at that stage, huh?"

Gannon lifted his hands out from his side. "Try to savvy how it was, Laredo. We thought you were out of it, did the only thing we could to make it legal for us to occupy this land."

"You and Drew."

"Yeah — me and Drew. We stayed pards for nigh on a couple years, then I had a chance to buy out this freight line cheap and Drew agreed it would bring us in money we could sink into the spread."

"The Star Bar by that stage, right?"

Gannon's eyes narrowed way down. "Well, you know Drew — easy-goin' as all get-out, hard worker, but no brains for the money side of things. I had to manage all the business . . . "

"And he was killed and now there's just you. No matter that I'm standing here in front of you after five years in the goddamnedest Mexican prison you ever saw . . . I come back and I don't have a share in any of this?"

"It's the way it is, Laredo," Gannon said quietly and his eyes were steady and there was a tone in his words that told Laredo he could talk from now till hell froze and it wouldn't change a thing. "Who you think built that lousy little piss-ant spread, your Double L, into the Star Bar empire, Laredo? Who you think sweated and busted a gut, borrowed money, gambled on every move turnin' out right? It was *me*, goddamnit! Not you. Far as I knew, you were pushin' up cactus from underneath somewhere down in Sonora. I didn't know you were alive. But what difference would it have made? I'm the one did all the work, built this place up to what it is." He shook his head. "No, I don't see you got any claim at all. Nor would any court."

Laredo was white under his dark skin, white with barely contained fury. "I got me one-third share coming from the sale of them mustangs. I've got my land that I proved-up on in the first place. I've got my cabin, still right where I built it, even if it has been worked into your damn stables. I've got a right to those things, Barr, and I aim to take them."

"Don't be a fool, Laredo. Look around you. How many men you think I've got working this place? Hell, I own all the land you can see from here clear to the horizon, twenty, thirty times as much as you had. I could squash you like a cockroach. All I've got to do is lift my finger . . ."

Laredo's hand went to his gun butt and there was a sudden stillness in the ranch yard. "You figure you can flick a finger before I get my gun out and

81

rking, Barr, why don't you go right ead."

The challenge was flung down boldly and Gannon's cold indifference was suddenly transformed into doubt and worry. Laredo had always been fearless, afraid of no man, and he had been fast with a six-gun, could knock out a turkey's eye at a hundred yards with a snapshot from his rifle.

Then suddenly Dancey kicked out from the steps, ramming his boot into the backs of Laredo's legs. They buckled violently and then Gannon was all over him, big fists swinging and pounding his head and body.

Laredo, used to sudden beatings by guards in Rebano, instinctively rolled into a ball, arms protecting his head. He huddled as boots drove into him and Gannon cursed him roundly.

"Uncover, you son of a bitch! Un-cover!"

Then Laredo took down his arms, straightened his legs and his body snapped like a bowstring as he leapt to his feet, met Gannon's rush, taking two blows on his forearms, then butted the man in the face. The rancher staggered and two of the hardcases, including Hi-spade, ran in and grabbed his arms. He came round easily with Hi-spade's pull and put an elbow against the man's jaw. It broke with a crack like a dry twig and he went down, slobbering spittle and blood, head pressed to the ground moaning as he held his slack jaw in both hands. The other man, the redhead, jumped back and started to reach for his gun but Gannon, his eyes still glazed a little, blood pouring from mouth and nose, shook his head. Ward Dancey waved Red back.

"Let 'em have a go-round," he said, glaring his hatred at the Texan.

Laredo stepped around Red and the man actually ran out of the way. Gannon was waiting and bared his teeth, driving a hard blow into Laredo's ribs. He grunted and staggered and the rancher took a long step forward, swinging both arms.

The Texan back-pedalled, parrying most of the blows but a couple slipped through and his head rang like a mission bell for the angelus. Dancey and Red and the other hardcase, Sweeney, yelled encouragement to their boss. Hi-spade, sick and spitting blood, crawled up on to the veranda and sat limply against the log wall, holding his jaw.

The Texan caught one of Gannon's fists in his palm, twisted the man's wrist brutally, bringing a startled yell to the rancher, lifting him to his toes. Laredo stepped in under the arm, drove his other fist up into the man's armpit.

Gannon gasped and his legs turned to water. He staggered and Laredo hit him again, this time on the side of the head. Gannon skidded down to one knee. Laredo's knee snapped his head back, almost breaking his neck. The rancher sprawled sideways, one hand dragging at his Colt. Laredo stomped on the hand, pinning it, looked down coldly through the sweat and the film of blood dripping into his left eye, and drove a boot into the man's ribs.

It sent Gannon rolling and as Laredo went after him, Dancey lunged from the steps, clubbed him to his knees with his gun butt, stepped around in front and bared his teeth as he lifted a knee under the Texan's jaw.

Laredo stretched out in the dust, clinging to consciousness by a hair. Eyes wild, Dancey glared at Red and Sweeney.

"Get the boss up!" He swung to look at Hi-spade and turned as some cowpokes came running up from the corrals to see what the ruckus was all about. He pointed to two of them. "Get Hi-spade into the sawbones. He's got a busted jaw."

Red and Sweeney were supporting the groggy Gannon between them and the rancher shook his head, blood flying, trying to clear his numbed brain. He frowned as he looked down at Laredo who was stirring on the ground.

But Dancey planted a boot between his shoulders and shoved his face down into the dust again.

"Want I should finish him, boss?"

Gannon swayed, took the kerchief Red handed him and mopped at his cut and bruised face. He stared at the blood on the cloth, dabbed at his smashed mouth, reeled a little as he kicked Laredo in the ribs.

"Not . . . yet," he panted. "He wants his land . . . right? OK, let's show it to him. Let him see how much it's changed since he . . . went to Mexico!"

The trio stared at him as Hi-spade was led away, moaning and slobbering. Gannon scowled.

"Dammit! Get me a rope!"

Ward Dancey holstered his six-gun and hurried into the house. He came back with a coiled lariat, held it out to Barr Gannon.

"Sit him up!"

Red and Sweeney dragged the semi-conscious Laredo to a sitting position and Gannon dropped a loop over the man's shoulders, ordered Dancey to pull the Texan's arms through and then yanked the rope tight into Laredo's armpits.

Laredo grunted and stared up with his one good eye. The left one was swelling fast and kept filling with blood from the cut above the brow. Gannon grinned bleakly at him.

"We're takin' you on a tour of your land, Laredo, ol' *compadre*! Laredo's Land you always called it. Well, it ain't your land no more, but I'll show you how I've improved it an' if you're still conscious when the tour's over, why, I might even tell you my future plans for it . . . Red, go saddle my black, Sween, you get hosses for yourself an' Ward. An' you, Laredo, you just set an' wait till we're ready to hit the trail."

He kicked Laredo hard in the side, laughing.

4

HE started to come out of it just about the time they were ready to go.

Laredo's head was spinning. His ribs felt as if they were all locked around his spine. There was a roaring in his ears and bright flashes behind his eyes.

He wondered when he had been caught in the buffalo stampede as he lurched drunkenly to his feet.

Something jerked and he staggered, almost fell to his knees, managed to stay upright. He shook his head once, sharply, gritted his teeth against the pain as his brain slopped around inside his skull, but found his vision and senses much clearer.

They had a rope on him, under his arms, and the end of it led to Barr Gannon who was sitting in the saddle of a big black gelding that must have stood seventeen hands. Laredo was pleased to see Gannon's face was battered and bruised, but that wasn't going to save him from what lay ahead.

"Just about to take you to see your land, Laredo," Gannon said, with an edge of bleak laughter to his words. "You know — what you call Laredo's Land? Only it ain't any more. But it could be — if you're buried there!"

He laughed and Ward Dancey and Red, also mounted, laughed with him. The black responded to the touch of Gannon's spurs and the rope snapped taut and Laredo lurched forward, stumbling wildly for a few moments before finding his feet. He trotted on behind the big black.

Gannon took it easy at first, going down-trail into the valley where the stream tumbled in a double waterfall. Laredo staggered and weaved along behind, hands gripping the rope which remained taut, never giving him enough slack to try to work on the slipknot of the loop. Besides, Dancey rode in close, keeping an eye on him, kicking him every few yards.

Gannon ran on with a kind of commentary, reminding the Texan of how his land used to look, pointing out his improvements — a small dam across the stream; diversion of the flow of one waterfall into a mid-level pasture, irrigating it so that the grass grew more lushly and could be used as winter feed; the blasting-through of a rocky spine between two low hills, an opening so that stock didn't have to be driven all the way around; clearing of brush and some timber which was utilized to build a small linecamp for the winter riders.

Laredo, despite his pain and near exhaustion, felt some admiration for Gannon. He had a good touch with the range, there was no doubt about that. Much better than the Texan would ever have believed.

Then they reached the wide stretch of pasture beyond the small valley and suddenly Gannon increased the pace forcing Laredo to run in order to stay on his feet. But he didn't stay upright for long.

The pace was too much. His legs couldn't keep up with those long, distance-eating strides of the black and Gannon laughed as he stumbled and fell, twisting, clinging to the bar-taut rope, trying to take some of the strain so it didn't cut too deeply into his chest and under his arms.

Gannon raked the gelding once more with the spurs. The black protested with a short whinny, snorted, lunged forward.

Laredo thought his whole upper body was being cut in two. His arms seemed to be ready to pop clear of their sockets. His body spun, a hip bouncing off a rock and drawing an involuntary cry from him.

"I guess you don't want to see this neck of the woods!" Gannon shouted over. "Too boring. So we'll just get through it quick as we can, OK, *compadre*?"

His laugh was lost in the thunder of hoofs as Dancey and Red rode on either side of the Texan who was almost lost in the cloud of dust and grit. He had rolled on his face now, spitting grit and squinting his eyes against the sting of gravel. His trousers and shirt were being torn as he was dragged roughly over the trail. But they weren't actually on the trail now, they had veered left and were cutting across country, through stunted brush and rock-studded slopes.

Laredo's body was being banged and battered and bounced every inch of the way. He lifted entirely off the ground every so often. The world rocked and jounced and swayed and spun. Vision faded, returned briefly, sometimes early enough for him to consciously wrench his body to one side and dodge a sharp rock or fanged bush. But not always.

Consciousness was slowly battered from him. The riders either side of him came in close, the hoofs thudding down within inches of his body. His fingers were bleeding, aching. His grip was weakening. The rope was cutting in deeper and would have been worse only for his buckskin shirt.

He was almost blind now with the stones cutting his face and blood running into its eyes to mix with the sand, making a sticky plaster he was unable to shake loose.

He couldn't breathe. He was choking, throat clogged with dirt. His head sagged forward. One hand fell away from the rope but he groped it back into position.

Minutes later it fell again, banged and battered and bounced over the ground. His body twisted. His shoulder struck and pain wrenched through him like a hot iron. His other hand lost the rope and his body began to twist helplessly, rolling and bouncing, causing Dancey and Red to veer aside so their horses didn't trample him.

"He's passed out, Barr!" yelled

Dancey, but if Gannon heard he made no response. Just kept on riding, dragging Laredo behind at the end of the ever-taut rope.

Until they reached the Rim standing high above the Tonto Basin.

Gannon hauled rein and the black blew and snorted and panted, rolling his eyes as he held it close to the edge. Dancey and Red approached cautiously, looking down at the ragged, bloody, dirt-caked figure at the end of the rope.

It was very still.

"Think you mighta finished him, Barr," Ward Dancey opined.

Gannon tripped in the saddle, hooked a heel around the saddle horn and began to build a cigarette with steady fingers. He had fired it up before he said casually, "Check him."

Red climbed down, looking some worried as he knelt beside Laredo. He rolled the man on to his back, grimaced at the torn and bloody clothing, the face that was caked with mud that was a mix of blood and dirt and grit. He leaned down, his ear close to the bloody mouth.

He looked a mite relieved when he glanced up at Gannon. "He's alive, boss."

Gannon grunted, went on smoking, looking out over the basin through the blue haze of distance, the green and silver of the land, rising up to the blue-black granite cliffs.

This was *his* land. He flicked his cigarette butt over the edge, settled into saddle and untied the rope from the horn. He flipped it to the ground and walked the black away, saying indifferently to Dancey, "Get rid of him."

Dancey frowned. "Where, boss?"

"Anywhere. Just get rid of him . . . I'm headin' into town for a few drinks and a little lovin'. Don't expect me back tonight."

Red frowned, watching Gannon riding down to the town trail without a backward glance.

"What you think he meant, Dance?"

Dancey scowled. "The hell you think?" He jerked his head at the edge of the Rim.

Red's eyes widened and he straightened, pale around the mouth as he shook his head. "Uh-uh . . . count me out! Judas, that'd be murder!"

Dancey's mouth twisted. "You're s'posed to be a hardcase."

"Shootin' a man's different. Judas, look at the poor son of a bitch. Five years in the worst jail in Mexico and he comes back to this!"

"You're goin' soft!"

"Mebbe . . . but if you want to push him over you do it without me. An' I'll have myself an alibi to say I was *never* here."

Ward Dancey frowned looking down at the unconscious Texan. He snapped up his head as Red started to move away.

"Hold up! You ain't leavin' me to do this alone!"

"Well, I sure ain't helpin' and I

don't care if you tell the boss or not. I'd rather lose my job than my life. Too many folk knew he was comin' to Star Bar."

Dancey scrubbed a hand around his jaw, wincing as he touched a tender spot. For a moment, determination flared in his eyes and he started to bend down towards Laredo, but stopped, glancing at Red.

"Hell, he's through here no matter what. He ain't gonna stick around these parts, even if he survives. Let's dump him over the edge of the trail yonder. It's above that sandy patch where we saw the mountain lion that time. Mebbe the cat'll finish him."

Red looked dubious. "I dunno, Dance — "

"Yeah you do." Dancey's gun was in his hand now. The barrel jerked, "Get the rope off him and we'll tote him up to the rocks and drop him over. Then we both hightail it to the other side of the spread and make damn sure the round-up crew savvies that we never left there all blamed day . . . You with me now?"

Red nodded. "I guess."

He wasn't too happy about any involvement at all but he figured since he'd gone along with it this far he might as well do the rest.

He knelt and began working at the tight knot on the noose that encircled Laredo's chest, the rope having cut so deeply into the flesh that it was barely visible.

★ ★ ★

There was glare and he moaned and rolled his head to one side without opening his eyes. That was better: it seemed to be more shaded this side.

It took him several seconds to realize that what his head rested upon was not the usual half-soft, half-stiff blanket folded over his saddle. It was much softer, much more comfortable.

That was it! It was *too* damn comfortable.

So he opened his eyes, slowly. It was bright and he squinted, immediately noting that his left eye only opened a slit anyway and felt heavy and larger than normal — not to mention mighty damn sore. But his right eye focused clearly enough and he saw he was in a room.

His brain was mush, all aswirl in his skull, pounding throbbing, reeling under a storm of thoughts. He closed both eyes again and his senses told him this was no cheap room in a saloon or rooming-house. Those had been good quality curtains tied back at the window and someone had cut out flower shapes from magazines or old calendars and pasted them on the half-lowered, brown-paper blind. He had noticed an Indian rug on the wall, glimpsed the corner of a dresser with some framed photographs and a lace cover.

This was someone's bedroom and the high ceiling told him it was likely in a ranch house. He struggled to sit up but there was so much pain and stiffness that he gave up quickly, grunting aloud. Panting, he raised his hands in front of his face, saw they were bandaged, and the bandages went halfway up his forearms. His chest felt constricted and he laboured to breathe and was just thinking about working up a yell — if he could find the strength — when he heard a door open.

He rolled his head that way, saw Teresa Backmann enter the room, looking anxious as she hurried to the bedside. She was wearing the same outfit as she had when he had seen her out on the Three Peaks trail — how long ago?

"I thought I heard a groan." She smiled and placed a cool, gentle hand across his forehead. He winced involuntarily as she touched the taped cut above his left eye. "Sorry. How do you feel . . . ? Oh, never mind. That's a foolish question after the way I found you."

His eyes asked "Where?"

"On a ledge below the Mogollon Rim. A mountain cat had been bothering some of our yearlings and I trailed it to a sandy ledge amongst some boulders. Its lair was probably close. But instead of finding the cat, I found you. Terribly torn-up and bloody. I thought you were dead."

She sat down on a chair and he noticed his gun rig with the Smith and Wesson dangling over the back. The holster was badly scratched.

Then it came back to him. The way Gannon had dragged him all those miles behind his big black . . .

"M-my . . . hoss . . . ?" he rasped and she got him a drink of water from a glass jug on the dresser and let him sip some before answering.

"One of my men found your roan and your packhorse wandering along the Rim. My guess is they were turned loose by whoever dragged you up to that ledge and threw you over."

Her eyes were blue and steady and he knew she was looking for answers.

But he wasn't quite ready to give any right now. He closed his eyes.

"So . . . tired," he slurred. "Thank you kindly . . . miss . . . but I . . . "

"That's quite all right. You get some sleep. You'll need a lot more before you're fit again."

"How . . . how long've I . . . ?"

"Been here? Two days. This is the morning of the third day. Now you rest. I'll leave one of Dad's walking sticks beside the bed. You rap on the floor or wall when you need me."

He didn't answer, heard her place the stick close to his head and then there was a brief silence before the door closed.

He'd intended to lie there and figure things out in his head, but overwhelming weariness sent him plunging deep into blackness where all thought was suspended.

The entire third day was one where he floated in and out of consciousness and everything had an unreal quality to it. The girl came to his room several times and once he recollected a stern, grey-stubbled man with faded rust-coloured hair and a nicotine-stained moustache: her father, Howard Backmann. He remembered little of any conversation, but the girl changed his bandages and, to his embarrassment, stripped him naked and washed him down without turning a hair.

He saw that she wanted to ask about his back but offered no explanation of the writhing snakes of scar tissue.

On the fourth morning he was ravenous and as sun was coming brightly in the window he groped for the walking stick and thumped it on the floor, realizing the ranch house must have two storeys.

But it wasn't the girl who came to him. It was a shy young Indian woman who smiled and nodded when he asked for eggs and bacon.

He ate everything the Indian girl brought him and mopped up the egg yolk and bacon grease with the last crust of bread, which he washed down with his third cup of coffee. Then Teresa appeared, wearing another checked shirt and baggy denim work trousers tucked into the tops of dusty half-boots.

"I think we can safely say you're on the mend now," she said, smiling at his clean plate.

"Good grub. Did I thank you yet for bringing me here?"

"Only about a dozen times so far. It seems I was wrong about you being a Gannon man."

The name sobered him and brought on his headache again. "Well, I thought we were pardners in Double L — the place he calls Star Bar now."

She sat on the edge of the bed. "You mentioned Double L that day I met you on the trail."

"It was my land. Six hundred forty acres, one full section, proved-up and deeded . . . I did that soon after the war ended. Then one day Gannon and another feller from Tennessee named Drew appeared. We'd ridden together in the army, chased down the Indians who were acting up while the war kept most of the army busy in the East. We'd always been good pards and they were broke and I took 'em in as equal pards on the Double L . . . "

His voice drifted a little as he recalled that time. It had been a good time, everyone full of vigour and enthusiasm, Gannon coming up with good suggestions, Drew keeping them entertained with his wild Blue Ridge Mountain stories and his harmonica.

Gannon had heard Maximilian down in Mexico was paying up to forty bucks a head for good horses. So they trapped mustangs, broke them in, and started driving them down to Maximilian's agent on the border, at Cisnero.

They had camped by Kettle creek, aiming to run the horses into Cisnero by early morning. Instead, they had been hit by bandits — not all Mexicans, either, because he had heard American voices yelling through the shooting.

The thunder and choking dust of a stampede whipped through the camp;

guns blazing; riders trying to run them under; men yelling as lead lifted them from the saddles.

Five, ten minutes of hell and din, no more, and the horses were gone and the churned ground was broken by the bulk of three bodies, one of which was still breathing.

It was Gannon who made him talk, swiftly, painfully. He told where the horses were being held and they left the man to die alone in his own blood, rode there and caught the rustlers on the hop.

They hadn't expected pursuit so soon, if at all. They had picked a canyon across in Sonora, one that Laredo knew well. In thirty minutes, they had all but a dozen of their horses back.

"That's fine!" Gannon had panted: he always tended to take control. "Let 'em have the rest. We've got over a hundred here."

"A dozen broncs are worth nearly five hundred bucks!" Laredo had said, still way up high from the action and the hard riding. "I don't aim to let that much go to them sonsabitches."

"I guess I'm with you, Laredo," said Drew, younger than the others, tending to need their approval in most things, so he looked at Gannon now.

But Barr Gannon had shaken his head. "Not worth the risk, *amigo*. You go ridin' around this country and no tellin' what you'll come up against."

"I busted a gut breaking in those horses," the Texan said stubbornly. "I ain't letting no Mex with gut-hook spurs make money out of them."

"The hell's it matter who gets 'em?" Gannon said irritably. "They just ain't worth the risk, not down here."

"I'm going — Drew, you stay and help Barr sell the others to that agent. I ought to be back in a couple days."

There might have been more argument but he had turned his already used mount and rode out at a fast clip . . . deeper into Sonora.

"Bad mistake," he told the sober-faced Teresa as she rolled him a cigarette, sitting on the edge of the bed. "*Federales* caught me after I got the horses back. I'd had to shoot it out with the three *bandidos* and they didn't like a *gringo* coming south of the border and killing their nationals. Things got a mite hot and smoky for a spell and I took down two *Federales*. So they threw me into Rebano prison for ten years." He smiled stiffly at the look on her face. "Guess I still owe 'em five or six."

She placed the cigarette between his lips, lit it for him, and sat back. "Is that where you got those scars on your back?" He nodded. She waited. He didn't explain. But she had enough imagination to know how it had been done.

"You've had a rough time of it, Laredo."

He shrugged. "Don't know any other way. Long as I can remember life's been a bi — been mighty tough." He gave her one of those brief smiles again. "So whenever you get something good you appreciate it more."

"You should smile more often. It makes you look ten years younger."

He smoked in silence. He knew she was waiting, so he told her how he had returned to Double L, his land.

"Leastways, that's what I thought. Now it's Star Bar and Gannon tried to kill me by way of welcome."

"What — what're you going to do now?"

"Soon as I'm well . . . "

"That won't be for weeks," she cut in and he snapped his head up.

"It won't be that long," he said, and went on before she could speak. "When I'm better, I guess I'm going to stick around a spell. And take back what's rightfully mine."

"You're a fool then! Barr Gannon will kill you. He's killed others — or his men have when he wanted land or a business and someone hasn't wanted to sell."

The Texan nodded slowly. "Barr always did have big ideas. Ought to've recollected that he told me once, not far from here come to think of it, up on White Mountain when we were tracking a bunch of 'Paches, he told me that when he settled down, he didn't just want a ranch, he wanted an empire."

She was very sober now and looked at him levelly as she said, "That's just what he's building. Over the bodies of innocent people." She was on her feet now and he saw she was edgy, worked-up about Gannon and his roughshod ways. "A few have tried to fight him. Most are dead. But one or two still hang about this area and harass Star Bar from time to time. Maybe you'd like to meet some of them?"

He frowned. "I dunno. Mebbe. But not yet a while. I need to get on my feet first. How long can I stay here?"

She faced him squarely. "If you're going to fight Barr Gannon, you can stay as long as you like."

He smiled thinly. "Reckon I won't ask how long I can stay if I just decide to ride on."

She gave him the smile back. "When you're ready, I'll escort you off Three Peaks land — with my shot-gun."

"Might even be worth it," he said quietly, not sure she heard him as she took the food tray away and left the room.

He sat there, propped up on a pile of pillows, smoking and making his plans.

Barr Gannon mightn't know it, but he was as good as dead. But not for a long, long time . . .

First, he had to be broken.

5

MOHAWK QUADE was caught flatfooted halfway across the creek at the southern end of his land.

He had taken a fancy for some fish and had seen a couple of bass in a hole under some shading willows and had made himself a pole and tied a piece of bright orange cloth over the bent wire hook for a lure. It would be fish for supper this night, but to reach the part of the pool where there was a ledge that the fish hid under, he had to remove his boots and wade on out. He left his rifle propped against the willow and that was his mistake.

He was a man of about fifty, hard as a horseshoe, and carrying four stone arrowheads in his lean body. He had himself a small parcel of land on one corner of the Rim, near the White

Mountain trail, and he figured to set out his days here, hopefully with some young squaw to take care of all his needs through the bitter winters.

He had yet to find himself that squaw, because folk around Sinola were mighty touchy about Indians. Their horses and freight wagons were often hit by Apache raiding parties. But no white woman would do for him what a squaw would.

So Mohawk made his cast with the water lapping mid-thigh and he felt the strike and he let out a rebel yell, jerked up the pole and thought he'd lassoed a runaway buffalo. The fish must be as big as a horse, he figured.

But he never found out.

He smelled the smoke first and he stopped his frantic wading as he went after the fish so abruptly the line snapped. Swearing, he looked around, saw his cabin on the ridge ablaze.

"Judas priest!" he breathed and began to wade ashore.

He stopped about halfway. Three

men suddenly appeared out of the shadows of the willows. Ward Dancey, Red and Sweeney. Dancey was holding Mohawk's rifle, worked the lever and checked there was a cartridge in the breech.

He grinned at the grizzled ex-army scout. "These old Henrys don't pack the punch of a Spencer or a new Winchester, Quade."

"Get outa here, Dancey!" Mohawk started to wade ashore, froze when Dancey fired and the bullet tore water in front of him. He knew it was too late to do anything about his cabin and his leathery lips tightened. "The hell're you doin'?"

"Guess you forgot what day it is," Dancey said. When Mohawk said nothing the big man sighed, levering another shell into the Henry's breech. "You're due to settle your account at the store."

Quade's jaw jutted. "Cheetham said I could let it ride another week."

Dancey shook his head. "When you

gonna learn that Cheetham's only a junior pardner now? Gannon's the man behind him and Barr says you've had enough time. You're two months behind already."

"So burnin' my cabin's gonna get him his lousy eighty-seven bucks?"

"Eighty-seven dollars and twenty-nine cents, Mohawk," Dancey corrected him. "No, we burned the hut because Barr don't want it."

"What . . . ? The hell with what Gannon wants . . . "

The rifle fired again and this time the bullet grazed Quade's leg and it buckled and he floundered in the shallows. Dancey nodded to Red and Sweeney and they quit leather in a hurry and before Mohawk had regained his balance, they were holding him by an arm apiece.

Dancey stood in front of him, holding the smoking rifle. "You're through here, Quade. Mr Gannon made you a fair offer but you spit in his face. He give you credit at his general store and the feed barn and you don't pay up on time, always gripin' for another week. So Mr Gannon's had a bellyful. He's takin' over your piss-ant spread, gonna incorporate it into Star Bar. You won't be needed."

"He can't do that! I proved-up on this place two years ago."

"But when you wanted that loan at the bank? For the dam on this here creek . . . ? You put up your place as collateral."

"With the *bank*, not Gannon!"

Dancey smiled coldly. "Mister, you are plain Injun dumb! Mr Gannon *bought* your lousy mortgage from the bank, see? So you got no place to live now. Your gear's gone in the fire. Boss said you could take one hoss and your guns, no ammo — when you come round, that is."

The rifle butt swung in a short savage arc into Mohawk's lean belly and he jack-knifed, gagging, but Red and Sweeney held him from falling. Dancey clipped him with the rifle's foresight, tearing the leathery face from jaw to hairline. Then he tossed the Henry into the creek, stepped forward, set his boots firmly, and methodically began swinging his hard fists into Mohawk Quade, hammering him from his midriff to his face and down again to his midriff.

★ ★ ★

"What kind of law you got around here?" Laredo asked when he heard about Mohawk Quade.

Teresa curled a lip. "Cliff Lindeen isn't exactly Gannon's man but he's weak and he's scared of Gannon."

The Texan nodded slowly, getting the picture.

"Gannon covers himself legally," put in Howard Backmann, sitting across the porch from where Laredo sprawled on a split cane lounge seat, taking some morning sun. He was stripped to the waist and the firm bandages encasing his ribs hid most of the scars on his

117

back. Cuts were healing, skin peeling, and bruises fading. Swellings had gone down but he was surprised at how weak he still felt. And something inside felt loose around his mid-section.

"He's got his fingers in so many pies in Sinola that most of the county is in debt to him in some way," added Howard.

"You folks?"

"No, *sir*!" said Backmann emphatically, his old eyes sparkling, his gnarled hands on top of the cane showing white knuckles. "We get along without puttin' ourselves in debt. What we can't pay for we don't have."

"It's what riles Gannon so much," Teresa said. "There's no way he can bring pressure to bear on us."

"Except through your crew," Laredo pointed out.

"Yes," she said soberly. "We've had men beaten, some driven off. There have been mysterious stampedes and fires, too, but nothing we could pin on Star Bar."

Laredo smoked thoughtfully for a spell, watching some of the Three Peaks cowboys breaking in some horses in the corrals. He felt a vague itch to be out there with them, but even moving to sit up cost him plenty of pain and he was short of breath.

"How about you folks make me out a list of everything that Gannon owns around here or that he has an interest in?" he said abruptly, earning sharp looks from father and daughter. Before they could ask what he wanted with such a list, he asked, "Where's this Mohawk now?"

"The doctor has him in his infirmary. He's not as badly hurt as you but he's older and he'll be a while recovering."

Laredo surprised her by smiling. "Old Mohawk might surprise you."

"You sound like you know him," opined Howard Backmann.

Laredo nodded. "We shared a can of beans a time or two when we hunted 'Paches."

"Speakin' of which," Howard said,

"there's word that Cougar and his bunch have hit the Tucson stage again. Seem to know just when that express box is full of gold."

The Texan frowned. "Cougar's the local bronco 'Pache, I take it?"

"Yeah. Well, not so local. His hideout's down in Sonora someplace. Some say he's part of Geronimo's crowd but I don't believe that. I reckon Cougar operates his own war agin the white eyes. They nearly got him when he hit the freight wagon near Fort Drago. Lieutenant swears he hit him, says his left arm was hanging by a shred when he rode off."

Laredo felt a prickling of his skin on the back of his neck. "When was this?"

"Aw, must be . . . " Backmann turned to the girl. "How long back since that fracas, Teresa? Couple months?"

"Not quite that long. About six weeks back, I'd say."

"Just about the time I made it back

across the border," Laredo told himself quietly. "By God, if that was Cougar I helped . . . "

He butted out his cigarette and flicked it into the yard. "Seems strange, Apaches going after gold. They'd rather kill settlers than tackle a stage or an army freighter."

Backmann made a wide gesture with his hands. "That's what's been happenin'."

"The army is afraid someone has offered them guns and the Apaches are getting money this way so as to pay for them," said Teresa.

Laredo frowned. "Could be. They'll take any kinda risk to get a hold of a repeating rifle — especially after the way they worked for Crazy Horse with Custer at the Little Big Horn."

"I hope you're wrong, Laredo," Teresa said, worry showing in her face. "If Cougar's war party were armed with Winchesters . . . my, I hate to think what might happen in this country."

Gannon was fuming, stalking back and forth across his office in his large ranch house, muttering curses. He heard footsteps out in the passage, wrenched open the door, startling Dancey and Red.

They took one look at the thunder-cloud face and both moved into the office warily. The rancher closed the door and leaned against it, his eyes blazing as they raked the two men.

"Laredo's alive!"

Dancey and Red exchanged glances. "Caint be, boss," Red stammered. "We threw him off the Rim."

Gannon lunged, catching Red unawares, smacked him across the face, open-handed. The crack was like a pistol-shot and Red staggered clear across the room, hit the corner of the desk and went down to one knee, dazed. Gannon spun towards Ward Dancey but the big man had stepped back, was crouched

122

a little, right hand hovering above his gun butt.

"Uh-uh, Barr — don't you try that with me!"

Gannon's face was gaunt, skull-like with his fury but something changed in his eyes. He always figured he was pretty damn fast with a six-gun but he *knew* how fast Dancey was. His jaw worked and slowly he calmed down, stepped around Red as the man pushed to his feet, one side of his face red and livid with the shape of Gannon's hand. The rancher poured himself whiskey, slopping it over the glass rim, tossed it down. He didn't offer any to the others.

"Almost three weeks that son of a bitch's been at Three Peaks and I've only just heard about it!"

"Like Red said, we tossed him off the Rim," Dancey said quietly, hand still close to his gun butt. "We dropped him over that ledge where the mountain lion has his lair. We figured if a mountain cat finished him off there

123

wouldn't be no evidence of what had happened to him here first."

Red was mighty leery of Gannon, stayed out of his reach, worked his way around so that he was close to the door and could make a fast getaway if necessary.

Gannon was calming down now, hitched a hip on to a corner of the desk. "Well, mebbe what you did makes some sense after all . . . but that goddamn Laredo! I've seen that stubborn son of a bitch stay on an Apache's trail for seven weeks straight. Last three we never cut a sign, but he was convinced the Injun was in the area and wouldn't quit. Thing was, this particular Apache had tortured one of Laredo's men to death and he wasn't about to let him get away with it. Starved him out in the end and Laredo fixed him good. Funny, though, despite him runnin' down dozens of 'Paches an' killin' 'em, he had a kinda admiration for 'em, use to say war and killin' an' huntin' was their way of life so we couldn't blame 'em for kickin' up a ruckus when we was takin' all their prime land." Gannon shook his head briskly. "He ain't gonna ride away from *his* land, I know he ain't."

They were silent: there didn't seem to be any profit in giving Gannon any kind of an answer.

The rancher raked his gaze from one man to the other. "You're slippin', too, Ward. I hear Mohawk's gonna be OK. He'll be ridin' again in about a week. 'Bout the same time Laredo'll be ready to ride. You got any idea what things'll be like around here if them two team up?"

Neither man said anything.

Gannon motioned that they could help themselves to a drink now and both men poured large ones. "What we gotta do is speed up our plans, make a move on Blewett's place and Old Man Zollinger's river ferry and so on. Get it all done before these two hardcases are fit enough to ride." He paused to pour himself another glass of whiskey. "Start with Blewett, Ward. Make good and sure that whatever you do to him will throw the fear of God into Zollinger. That way we won't have so much trouble when we get around to him."

Dancey smiled, relaxing at last. "Sounds like there ought to be a bonus in this."

Gannon laughed. "You've got your gall, Ward! But, OK — hundred bucks."

Dancey grinned but Red didn't lose his worried look and led the way back towards the corrals. Halfway he stopped and Dancey looked at him puzzledly.

"How come you're steppin' on your chin? You'll get a bonus, too."

Red rubbed at his sore face. "Not me, Dance — 'cause I'm ridin' out."

Dancey stiffened. "Quittin'? You gone yeller?"

Red shook his head. "I dunno, to be honest, Dance, I just got this real bad feelin' ridin' me. Sween an' me've been talking it over for some time."

"Sween, too? You're a couple old ladies. You both take Barr's money quick enough."

"What good's money if you're in the Yuma Pen? You know what I think? I reckon Barr's scared white of this Laredo. He knows he done him wrong and he knows Laredo ain't gonna let him get away with it. He panicked once, draggin' him behind that rope and then orderin' *us* to throw him off the Rim. He's jumpy again now an' he's gonna push us into takin' all kinds of risks . . . even straight-out murder."

Dancey's face was rock hard. "We're bein' paid to take risks — I shouldn't've listened to you up on the Rim that day, then we wouldn't have this trouble with Laredo."

"Well, you do what you want, Dance. But I'm goin'. Gannon can keep what money I got comin'. I dunno if Sween's gonna quit, too, but I sure am. *Adios*, Dance."

Dancey stood and watched Red hurry towards the bunkhouse. The man was running scared, all right.

"You keep your mouth shut!" he called. Red spoke over his shoulder. "I'll keep mum. If I don't I'll only get myself into a heap of trouble, won't I?"

Dancey ran his tongue around the inside of his lower lip. "Yeah," he said almost to himself. "A heap of trouble — and mebbe even if you *don't* open your mouth . . . "

6

DOCTOR MARCUS LITTLE marvelled that someone as old as Mohawk Quade could recover from such a beating so quickly. And completely.

"Comes of good livin', Doc," Quade told the doctor, winking. His leathery face would bear the scar of the gunsight until he died but the bruises and swellings would fade. He was limping and favoured his ribs some but he was eager to leave the medic's small infirmary behind the street-front office.

"I got me some chores to do, Doc."

Little was anything but: he was six-four and weighed well over 200 pounds; floors shook and creaked under his heavy boots. He had huge hands that were amazingly gentle and whiskers seemed to sprout all over his moon face.

The small pebble-lens spectacles that he wore gave him a comical look but his manner was always gruff and few had seen him smile. But everyone knew that gruff manner hid a soft heart.

"Mohawk, you don't even have a ranch. What kind of chores could be taking you out of your bed so blamed soon? *Too* blamed soon."

"Special chores, Doc."

"Now, you listen to me, you fool Indian fighter. Those days are gone. You ought to be taking things easy now in the winter of your life."

"Winter be damned! Fall, mebbe, but I'll see another summer before I kick off, Doc."

He gathered his few things, including the Henry rifle that had had a broken stock when they had brought him in but which the gunsmith had fixed while Quade had been abed.

Little placed a large hand on his arm. "Mohawk, we've known each other a good many years. A couple of those arrowheads you carry are on the move, one near your spine. If it touches the spinal nerve — well, you'll be paralysed."

That stopped Quade in his tracks. He frowned. After a silence he said quietly, "Doc, as long as I can move one arm and my trigger finger, paralysis won't have time to bother me."

"Damnit, Mohawk! Show some sense. You go scooting all over the territory and one of those arrowheads could yet kill you."

"Well, we'll see, Doc. You like to take a bet on how long it might take?"

"You're a fool! Get the devil out of my house!"

Quade smiled. "I'll drop a deer on your back stoop in payment, Doc. I don't have no money."

"Go on. Be stupid."

But Mohawk had only reached the passage when Teresa Backmann came hurrying in, stopped briefly to ask after the old scout's health and looked at the doctor.

"I have Laredo outside in the buckboard. He's having trouble with his lower ribs. I think one may be broken."

"Damn well should have called me in the first place," Little grouched, but went for his bag. "Mohawk, if you're feeling so spry, help Teresa bring that Texan in here."

Laredo limped in to the infirmary, the girl on one side, Quade on the other. He nodded to the waiting medic.

"It's nothing, Doc. I didn't want to waste your time but Teresa . . . "

"Be quiet. I'll be the judge if you're wasting my time or not," Little snapped, and pushed the girl aside and Quade too, lifted Laredo — no light weight — on to the padded table. The Texan grunted. "Well, your screams didn't lift the roof so I'm sure your rib's not broken. Maybe just cracked."

He went to work with Teresa and Quade waiting. The doctor pressed and squeezed, bringing sweat to Laredo's face and making him catch his breath

132

sharply. He shook his head.

"No breaks. Just badly bruised. I can still see the shape of the boot in that fading bruise." He looked down at the Texan. "You were such a quiet man when you were here before. I don't think I ever remember you in a brawl."

Laredo smiled crookedly. "Wouldn't call this a brawl, either, Doc. More like a beating."

Little grunted and proceeded to bind the man's lower ribs tightly with wide, firm bandages, enlisting the girl's aid. Quade moved to where he could see Laredo's face.

"Been a few years since that manhunt down in Chihuahua."

"Yeah. You run into a door, Mohawk?"

"Not unless doors've got names. This one'd be Dancey."

Laredo nodded his jaw towards his bruised body. "Thought you might recognize his signature."

Quade nodded, grim-faced. "Burned

me out, run off my stock, beat-up on me and stole my land. Legal. Gannon bought up my mortgage from the bank."

Teresa snapped up her head. "That's contemptible!"

"Mebbe, but he done it. Run me off with my hoss and my Henry but no ammo — "

"If you want a place to stay, Mohawk, you're welcome at Three Peaks," the girl offered.

"Why thank you kindly, Teresa. But I stay with you and it'll only bring more trouble for you."

She frowned. "Why? It's none of Gannon's business who stays on my ranch."

Quade glanced at Laredo. "I aim to stick around the Mogollon. But I also aim to be kinda busy."

The girl still looked puzzled although the Texan savvied what Quade meant.

Sourly, Doc Little said, "He's talking about harassing Gannon, the old fool."

Teresa was shocked. "Mohawk, I'm

134

not sure that's a good idea."

"Good or not, he ain't gettin' away with burnin' me out." He looked at Laredo. "How soon you be up and around?"

"Soon as Doc ties off these bandages."

"Ridiculous! Whatever makes you Texans think you're cast in an iron mould? You try to ride and you could very well crack that rib and have it pierce a lung."

"You said there were no breaks, Doc, only badly bruised. I've had five years in a Mexican jail. I've crushed rock with a fourteen-pound sledge with worse wounds than this. Had to, or I'd've been shot."

"Well, no one's going to shoot you now if you show some sense and rest up and let nature take its course," snapped Little, and the girl backed him, trying to talk Laredo into showing some good sense.

"Mohawk and me've got some chores to do," the Texan said. "Sooner we get started the better."

She looked appealingly at the big medic but he only shook his head.

"I learned a long time ago it's no use arguing with a stubborn Texan — and this one here is about the stubbornest I've come across."

"You haven't got your guns," Teresa said with a touch of triumph, but Laredo smiled.

"I had your wrangler — Manolo — pack 'em in the buckboard under the blankets. By now, he'll have my roan and packhorse stalled at the livery. Told him they were your orders. You don't mind, do you?"

Teresa flushed and stamped her foot. "Oh!"

Little sighed. "At least rest up for a couple of hours, give yourself time to recover from the buckboard ride in."

Laredo was going to protest, but nodded. A little give wouldn't hurt any and he had to arrange for stores and so on. But Quade could get that all done for him.

Mohawk agreed readily. "You mind

if I buy some Henry ammo, too?" Laredo shook his head. "OK — how about we have a drink at the Broken Corral later?"

Laredo said that would be fine and Mohawk left. The girl seemed as if she wanted to say something to him, but shook her head and took her leave.

The Texan called, "Thanks for everything, Teresa."

She looked back, hand on the door knob. "I've a feeling it's all been wasted effort!" Then she stomped out.

Doctor Little gathered his things. "She could be right. That man, Hi-spade, whose jaw you busted . . . he quit you know. First Star Bar man ever to run out on Gannon. It'll be just one more thing he'll hold against you."

"Won't keep me from sleeping, Doc."

Then Teresa, pale and worried-looking, came hurrying back into the infirmary.

"My God! I don't know what this place is coming to. They're

just bringing in Keg Blewett's body. Seems he was attacked and killed by Red Hooks. But he managed to shoot Red before he died. That Mexican who works for him found them lying sprawled in the ranch yard. He'd been out tending Keg's stock on the range."

As she spoke there was the sound of voices at the side door and the doctor strode across. Men came bustling into the room, surrounding the staggering old Mexican carrying the limp, blanket-wrapped body of Keg Blewett. But two townsmen followed, toting Red Hooks's body between them, one of his hands dragging along the floor.

Doc Little snapped angrily at the men as he lifted Red's trailing hand, "Have some respect for the dead, for God's sake!" He cut off the last word and his face changed and Laredo struggled to sit up on the table.

"What's wrong, Doc?"

Little frowned, still holding Red's hand. He bent over the body briefly and straightened, looking at the Mexican who had laid Blewett on the table. "You say Red shot your boss, Juan?"

"*Si, señor*. I find in yard, only three metres between. Red he shot twice in back, *jefe* have gun in his hand."

"Well, he might've shot Red, but Red didn't shoot him — Hooks has been dead at least twenty-four hours longer than Keg."

* * *

Sheriff Cliff Lindeen was called in but no one expected much from him. He was a young lawman with a young wife and a child not quite four years old.

He was a man who trod carefully, maybe not exactly corrupt, but willing to cut corners if it would keep trouble at bay. 'Trouble' meaning if he didn't have to stir things up by going up against the powerful people in Sinola. And the most powerful of all, of course, was Barr Gannon.

Immediately he recognized Gannon's

hand in this although there was talk around town — started by Dancey and other Star Bar hands — that Red Hooks and Blewett had been arguing over a horse Blewett supposedly sold Red. Red had complained it was only half broken and there were witnesses that he had been thrown several times.

The story was that it had happened up on the open range and it had been one time too many. It had to be conjecture after that but it would seem that Red had come down to Keg Blewett's to have it out with him and it had escalated to gun play.

"Seems straightforward then," the sheriff opined, his young face flushed. He sported a stringy moustache in an attempt to make himself look older and he tugged a mite nervously at it now.

"Except if you swallow that Star Bar story about Red, Blewett was killed by a man who'd already been dead for twenty-four hours," growled Doc Little.

Lindeen seemed mighty uncomfortable. "Look, it don't make sense, Doc. I've asked around town — there are some Star Bar men in right now — and Red was seen yesterday, complained to Ward Dancey about being thrown and said he was going to have it out with Blewett. Ward tried to stop him, but . . . "

"Gannon has always wanted Blewett's place," said Teresa. "Everyone knows that Gannon aims to drive out the nesters and take all that river bottom land into Star Bar. He's been making them ridiculous offers for ages. Keg Blewett is closest to the Star Bar line so he'd be first to go."

"That could make sense, Teresa," Laredo said and the sheriff flushed again.

"Look, you people are making all this up. There's no proof. Until you have something to back your theories, I suggest you keep quiet before you get into trouble." Lindeen seemed very uneasy. "I can't accept your theory, either, Doctor, about Red."

"Out!" roared Little, causing the startled lawman to step back hurriedly. "Out of my infirmary and don't come back unless you need my attention — and then you might wish you didn't! You're a stupid man, Cliff Lindeen."

Lindeen's lips were white and his eyes flashed, but although he hesitated, he suddenly swung towards the door and hurried out.

"Idiot!"

"Keg Blewett was murdered," insisted the girl. "If not by Gannon himself, then certainly on his orders."

"No one'll ever be able to prove that, Teresa," Laredo told her quietly. "Barr's a smart man. None too ethical, but damn smart. Red'll be blamed for killing Blewett, you see."

"Well, something has to be done — and I really think things around here have speeded-up since your return."

"Something'll be done, all right. Mohawk and me'll see to that."

Alarm showed on the girl's face.

"What are you planning? And where will you stay?"

Laredo gestured vaguely. "We both know the hills pretty well."

"Crawling with Apaches," warned Little and Laredo smiled slowly.

"We both know Apaches pretty well, too, Doc."

★ ★ ★

As they rode out of town, Laredo hunched-over some in the roan's saddle, with Mohawk riding alongside leading the line-backed dun which carried their packs, Dancey and Sweeney and a couple of other Star Bar hands appeared on the porch of La Salle's old saloon. One of them spat. Dancey propped a leg on the porch rail as he rolled a cigarette, hard eyes watching the riders in the late afternoon glow.

"Two old cripples lightin'-out with their tails tucked up between their legs," he said loudly and the Star Bar hands guffawed.

"How far you figure they'll make, Dance?"

"Aw — 'bout as far as I decide to let 'em."

Mohawk casually swung his Henry across his thighs, the muzzle tracking the group as his dappled grey plodded by.

"I got me some ammo again, Dancey," the old scout said quietly but the words carried to the ramrod and he paused licking the cigarette paper. "Leave it, Mohawk," Laredo told him. "Time enough for squaring-away later."

Dancey grinned. "Much later if I know you two."

Above the raw laughter, Laredo said. "That's something for you to think on, Dancey. *Do* you know us? Huh?"

Dancey's face was a study in bewilderment as they rode on towards the edge of town. Sweeney, very quiet, sober, said, "I'm goin' to see about a headboard for Red — anyone comin'?"

144

They stared at him silently and his mouth tightened. "Figures," he murmured and swung away along the boardwalk, shoulders stiff, his stride jerky.

Damn! He wished he'd quit a couple of days ago when Red had said he was going. They had been pards for more than ten years. Might not have stayed on the right side of the law all that time, but they had been as close as damnit to being real friends, closer than most men who rode the trails they had followed . . . but he'd been too *scared* to quit . . .

Now Red was dead, used right up to the last by Gannon and Dancey.

And, he told himself savagely, big hands clenching as he made his way into the lumber yard for a slab of pine, *you're still scared, you yeller bastard!*

★ ★ ★

Mohawk knew these hills better than Laredo, took him to a tumbledown cabin in a grassed and watered canyon that gave a view out over the Rim and the basin if a man wanted to climb a little way.

They chased out a couple of rats and the snake that had been preying on their brethren and, by candle light, Mohawk fixed up the bunks so they could spread their bedrolls.

Laredo's side was giving him some hell and he had the old scout adjust the bandages and then Mohawk brewed his 'six-gun' coffee — which meant it was strong enough to float such a weapon — and indifferently fried-up sowbelly and opened a can of beans.

Laredo ate mechanically: it was lousy grub but there was nothing like a Mexican prison diet to make a man appreciate even half-way decent greasy food.

"Got me a list here of places around that Gannon either owns or has an interest in." Laredo handed the paper that Teresa had made out to Mohawk

Quade but the man didn't even look at it.

"Know most of his interests. An' he got nearly all of 'em by bein' tough or just ridin' roughshod over the original owners." Quade stared into the fire, took out his corncob pipe and began to fill it with tobacco Laredo had paid for. "There's a lot of places. Which ones you figure we hit first?"

"I was wanting you to help pick one out from the list."

"Well, there's that saloon in Sinola, Cheetham's Emporium, that's mostly Gannon's — poor old Cheetham's only there to run it. Or you got the feed and grain store, a cathouse down Powder Lane, some frame houses goin' out by the river. Not to mention all that range he's got cows and broncs runnin' on." He grinned suddenly, showing stained yellow stumps of teeth through the screen of whiskers. "We can keep ourselves amused right through winter!"

"Don't want it to take that long,

Mohawk. There's his freight business, too. Maybe we could hit a couple of his wagons just to get things going."

The scout looked disappointed. "Hell, I reckon we're gonna do anythin' at all, make it a grand start!"

The Texan smiled, rubbing gently at his aching side. "You could be right. Well, we've got time to think about it yet." He lurched to his feet, making for the bunk. "I'm turning in. This damn side's giving me hell."

Over breakfast Laredo asked, "Know this Apache, Cougar, who's been tearing up the countryside lately?"

Mohawk, crouched before the fire-place, glanced over his shoulder. "I know him. Tangled with him three-four times. Meaner'n Geronimo."

"What's he look like?"

The scout frowned. "Tall for an Apache, all muscle and sinew, face as broad as a dinner plate, big nose, favours a red headband, got a scar from a sabre up behind his right ear. Lucky to still have his head, but that day the cavalry man who slashed him, hit him with the back of the blade. What's wrong, *amigo*?"

Laredo looked up, a mite haunted. "I think I helped him down in Sonora." He told Quade about finding the wounded Indian threatened by the floodwaters.

Mohawk shook his head slowly. "Man, you best keep it to yourself. You won't win no friends this side of the border if they know you helped Cougar. I ain't too surprised, though. You'd hunt 'em down and kill 'em quick as anyone else, but you still figured they had a right to fight us, din' you?"

Laredo shrugged. "We stole their land. We made 'em promises, never even tried to keep 'em. You'd fight, wouldn't you, under those circumstances?"

"Yeah. I got respect for the ol' 'Pache, too, but I never got used to seein' white folks who were just tryin' to make a life for themselves slaughtered like a pack of rabid wolves

149

had got in amongst 'em."

"Why you think Cougar's stealing gold?"

That gave the scout pause for a few moments. "Must need money for somethin' — guns, ammo, whiskey — yeah, he's buyin' somethin' with that gold. Repeaters'd be my guess."

Laredo thought the same. "In Wildman Creek, I was almost run down by one of Gannon's wagons. Dancey was driving. Seems odd, a ranch foreman driving a freight wagon."

"Usin' the wagons to get the guns to the Injuns! Hell, it makes sense — and Gannon's wagons are hit once in a while but mostly his men seem to get away unharmed. Could be a way of deliverin' the guns. But why would he risk that? Gannon's gotta live up on the Muggyown, too."

"And he's trying to grab it all — a heap of settlers have been scared out of their wits by the Indian raids. Howard Backmann told me a lot had quit the Rim and basin and Gannon moved in right away to get their land cheap or at no cost. Could work out pretty good for him. Get paid for the guns, then pick up what land he wants after Cougar and Geronimo scare off the settlers."

A slow smile creased Quade's already lined face. "I always did like workin' for you on them manhunts, Laredo — you got a notion, you followed it through. Got you in a heap of trouble with your officers but I never heard of any of 'em who didn't take the credit when you was right. Which was most of the time."

"We need to watch for Dancey driving one of the freight wagons. If I'm right, he'll only do it when they've got something to deliver — or pick up."

"I got a couple friends around town who'll handle that for us, let us know when Dancey's on a wagon."

"OK. Now, we get some rest today and tonight we let Gannon know we're still around."

"Suits me. But first I ride down to Zack Zollinger, he runs the ferry at the crossin'. He can tell us just about where everyone is on the Rim because there ain't no other way to cross the river for twenty miles. Gannon's got land on both sides so Zack'll know how many men are workin' where."

"Take it easy," Laredo said, wondering if this ache in his side was ever going to go away.

It seemed to be worse since Mohawk had adjusted the bandages. Maybe the old scout was right: he should leave the bandages sit, instead of loosening and trying to tighten them all the time.

Turning on his good side, he pulled up the blanket and tried to sleep. But it eluded him. He was too keyed-up, eager to start paying back Barr Gannon for his betrayal.

By the time he was through, Gannon would wish he had never heard of Laredo.

7

THERE was trouble down at the ferry and Mohawk Quade adjusted the focus on the field glasses Laredo had given him, raking the lenses across the activity below at the river.

It was wide and deep here, but with good easy approaches on either side and because it widened the current was not so strong. There were trees on both banks, affording good anchor points for the cables and ropes and Zollinger and his sons had built cabins on both banks.

The first thing Quade saw was that the main cabin, on the bank below his vantage point, had been burned down, the fire taking a couple of the ponderosa trees with it. There were three freight wagons lined up down there, Star Line, of course, and men milled about, fighting the teams and pushing the wagons one at a time on to the wide raft of the ferry.

Swinging the glasses to the far bank, he saw more Star Bar men waiting, one wagon already across, the team being hitched up again. He tried to make out the driver, wondering if this was one of the special times when Dancey took the reins, but he couldn't see the man who climbed on board.

He sniffed and smelled the damp stench of charred timber, figured the fire had taken place a day or so beforehand. His mouth was grim: there was no sign of Zack Zollinger or his burly sons. One had been married to a young Yaqui squaw who was pregnant last time he had seen her, but she wasn't around, either.

Well, looked like he had to get down there and find out what in hell had happened. He had a pretty damn good idea but he wanted details and his hand already itched where he gripped his battered old Henry rifle.

Then it was too late.

Someone had spotted the sun flashing off the field glasses. Men were turning at another's shout and he pointed directly at Mohawk's position. The old scout cussed as he slid back immediately, scrabbling down off his rock, losing the Henry at one stage and cussing even harder. The Henry rifle's big fault was its under-barrel tubular magazine. It was made only of tin and dented far too easily. Just one dent could foul-up the feeding of cartridges to the breech and, sure enough, the tube was dented a few inches from the breech end. With a cartridge already in the breech, he figured he would be able to lever in two more at most, then the others would jam.

Fine time for something like that to happen.

By then he was swinging into the saddle of the dappled grey and three riders were charging up from the ferry. He wheeled and hit the trail into the rocks, two bullets singing off boulders behind. He wouldn't be able to waste his ammunition. He had to ride like hell and hope to outdistance pursuit. With the damaged rifle, there was no sense in figuring on a shoot-out.

They scattered, two riding hell for leather for a low slope that would allow them to cut across his present trail ahead of him. He wheeled left and immediately saw that this was what they wanted: there was a drop there, almost straight down, and a man would have to be riding Pegasus to get down that way.

The third man, hard on his heels, cut left too, but lower down, then angled back up in a dip that made it a lot easier on his horse, a black with a streak of white down his neck. Mohawk knew who that was: Sweeney rode a horse like that, and he would dearly love to tangle with that sonuver. It had been Sweeney and Red who had held him while Dancey beat the crap out of him.

He whirled completely around, taking

them all by surprise, spurred the grey back the way he had come. It left his pursuit caught way out near the steep drop-off. Sweeney was closer in but still farther back than previously.

Rifles hammered in fury but he only heard a couple of bullets thunk into the slope. They were shooting too low.

A faint yell reached him above the rush of wind past his ears.

"Nail him, Sween!"

Mohawk glanced back, saw Sweeney sweeping back to the original trail and coming fast. The other two had been caught flat-footed and knew it was hopeless for them to try to make up the ground they had lost. They sat their mounts, rifles in hands, watching as Sweeney desperately tried to close the gap.

Mohawk twisted and turned and cut through boulder fields where no man would normally race a horse, but Sweeney kept coming. Twice he yelled something and triggered a few times but Mohawk didn't look back, kept going, crouched low.

The climb steepened. The grey began to blow hard, sweat making its coat dark and slick. Mohawk had chosen a no-trail way of getting into the hills and now he rode in behind a group of rocks like the spread fingers of a hand and slid from the saddle.

Mohawk settled himself beside his finger rock, bracing his arm against the gritty surface, trying to put the foresight squarely on Sweeney's chest. But the man was hunched over some, juggling the reins, and Mohawk couldn't get a clear shot. Patiently, he waited. There was a smooth section of about three yards and a space between two of the boulders at the halfway mark. He set the Henry's sights there and waited.

The black's head showed first, moving more easily now on the clearer ground underfoot, and Sweeney appeared, rifle carried in one hand, urging the horse quickly past the gap. But not fast enough.

Mohawk's Henry cracked and Sweeney

went out of the saddle as if struck by a falling tree. The black whinnied and ran on, hidden by the rocks. But Mohawk could still see Sweeney, scrabbling on the ground, trying to drag himself into cover. The scout stood, rifle firmly to his shoulder, breathing shallowly, then not breathing at all as he steadied the rifle on the wounded man and put a second shot into him.

Sweeney was driven against the earth and Quade saw the puff of dust from under his face as the lead smashed the breath from him. Mohawk levered, felt the resistance, strained at the lever and then the soft copper rimfire cartridge squeezed past the dent in the tube and fed into the hot breech. The breath hissed softly through his teeth.

Sweeney had rolled in behind some rocks and from his vantage point, Mohawk could see the blood spattering the ground. He felt good about that because there was a lot of it.

He ought to just ride away, just leave the man there to die slowly,

Quade thought, but it would be nice to know what the hell had happened to the Zollingers. They had been good friends to him over the years, rarely charged him for using the ferry, fed him, staked him when he was broke. He figured he owed them something. So he started making his way down to where Sweeney lay. He moved as quietly as any Indian, instinctively choosing cover and a track that would bring him to a point where he would be lower than the wounded man and could approach from behind him.

He heard the man's breathing when he was still five yards away, wet, bubbling, interspersed with gasping. Lung-shot, he reckoned.

Eager now to get there, Mohawk clambered over some low rocks but froze when he suddenly found himself looking down the muzzle of Sweeney's rifle.

The man, blood running from his twisted mouth, his shirt-front red, glared at him, wild-eyed, getting ready to die.

The old scout swallowed, waiting for the bullet that at last had his name on it.

* * *

Laredo heard the horse coming and swung his legs off the bunk, catching his breath sharply as he snatched up his rifle. He crouched by the window, looking out through the partly open shutter and saw the lone rider coming slowly into the hidden canyon.

Mohawk.

Laredo opened the door and waited while Quade corralled his weary grey. The scout pushed past the Texan without speaking, went straight to the whiskey bottle he had bought with Laredo's money in Sinola and took a deep swig.

"Wondered if you were gonna make it back before dark," Laredo said quietly, moving into the cabin. He

161

took down the sowbelly and began slicing some into the skillet.

"Gannon's got the ferry," Quade told him.

Laredo's head snapped up. "Your friend — Zollinger?"

"Dead. One of his sons wounded. But Gannon let him go with his brother and his Injun wife — after they signed the ferry over."

"What's Barr want the damn ferry for?"

"Only one there is and it's twenty miles up or downstream to another crossin'. Folk want to use the ferry, they gotta pay whatever he asks now. But it ain't the money: it's the control. Gannon brings the freight to Sinola and other towns along the Rim. They're dependent on him for supplies. He won't let any other traders through, you can bet on that. Now he's got the monopoly."

Laredo allowed *that* sounded more like Gannon. Then he frowned. "How'd you get the details?"

"They spotted me. Two dropped out but me and Sweeney had a sort of go-round and I nailed him twice. But he got the drop on me and I thought for sure I was a goner. Instead, he said he wanted to talk with me before he cashed in his chips."

"Talk?"

Quade nodded. "Seems Red tried to quit Star Bar. But no one does that. Dancey rode after him and next day Red's found dead at Blewett's and everyone figured he shot Keg over some hoss they was s'posed to be arguin' about, and Blewett nailed Red. Tied it up neat as Christmas."

"Where's Sweeney now?"

"Dead. Lung-shot. He ain't no loss. He was one of the bastards held me while Dancey altered my looks."

"Sounds to me like Gannon's ready to run hog-wild." Laredo poured coffee and flicked some greasy bacon strips on to two tin plates. He pushed one towards Mohawk Quade and sat down across the table from him. "One thing,

163

we don't have to think twice about what we're gonna hit tonight."

★ ★ ★

There were four Star Bar men guarding the ferry station on the south bank of the river when Laredo and Quade got there. They had built a camp-fire near the charred ruins of the Zollinger cabin and were seated around it, drinking from a flat bottle of rotgut whiskey that was passed from hand to hand.

Mohawk, beside Laredo, nudged him and held up a hand, pointing across the dark river, arching his eyebrows, shrugging.

Laredo shook his head — he couldn't tell how many men might be on the far bank. But the ferry was moored at this side.

Through brief sign language, Laredo indicated how Mohawk was to move into position. He glanced back at the men and by the time he had turned around, the old scout had gone. They had worked on his Henry after supper with a carefully whittled stick pushed into the dented tube and then used the rounded butt of Laredo's Smith and Wesson to tap out the damage. The ammunition now fed smoothly into the chamber.

Laredo moved around to the right, climbing a little higher into the deep shadow of the ponderosas. Sycamore threw weird patterns between him and the fire. He settled, drew bead on the flat whiskey bottle as a man he knew only as Lobo passed it to the Mexican beside him. The rifle crashed and the bottle shattered simultaneously, fiery liquor flaring in a ragged flash as it spilled into the flames.

Lobo and a Mexican tumbled back off their log in alarm and the other two leapt to their feet. Laredo put three fast shots into the fire, scattering coals and burning sticks. The men on their feet grabbed at their guns and Mohawk came out of the darkness behind them, clubbed one to his knees with the Henry's butt and backhanded the other, sending him staggering. By the time he and Lobo and the Mexican had recovered their senses, Laredo and Mohawk had them covered and the fourth man groaned sickly where he lay on the ground.

Mohawk moved quickly behind the men and removed their handguns, tossing them into the dark river.

"You won't walk away next time we get our hands on you, Quade!" growled Lobo.

Mohawk swung his Henry casually and the heavy barrel laid across Lobo's head and dropped him on the spot. The Mexican and the other conscious white man watched with wide eyes.

Laredo jerked his gun barrel. "Start dragging some of that charred timber out on to the raft. Pile it up big, then set fire to it."

They stared, mouths agape, and Mohawk reinforced Laredo's orders by rough jabs of his rifle barrel. As the men moved to obey reluctantly, voices called from across the river.

"The hell's all the shootin'?"

"Lobo? Quintana? You OK?"

"Sure," called back Mohawk, slurring his voice, "Whiskey bottle fell in the fire an' blew up, scared us white. We started shootin' at nothin' . . . "

There was a laugh and a voice said, "An' you're drinkin' that stuff . . . ? *Hey!* The hell you doin' with the fire? Jesus!"

The fire was blazing up now in the centre of the raft. Laredo ordered the Star Bar men to pile on more timber. Mohawk prowled the ferry, searching under a smelly tarpaulin. He found a large can of grease which was used on the cables and pulley wheels. He made the Mexican smear large dollops of it on the timbers. It spat and crackled and flared.

The men across the river were through yelling now and started shooting. Laredo saw that the mooring rope was stretched bar-taut and knew men over there were trying to pull the raft across.

The fire was really blazing by now and none of them could approach closer than six feet because of the heat.

Mohawk muscled the Gannon men ashore and Laredo cut the mooring rope. It parted with a dull twang and he could imagine the cusses of the men across the river as they fell when the resistance suddenly went. The ferry began to move out into the river, blazing from end to end.

By the time it reached the middle, the guide rope would have burned through and the raft would start its slow but inevitable journey to extinction.

★ ★ ★

Barr Gannon stared in disbelief as Lobo and the other crestfallen river guards brought him the news about his newly acquired ferry.

The rancher's hair was tousled and he wore only his underwear, having been awakened by Lobo's hammering on the ranch house door. Now he stared at his men blankly for several long seconds.

"Great God A'mighty!" he breathed finally, truly stunned. "The ferry's . . . gone?"

"Right down river, boss, burnin' like the Fourth of July." Lobo assured him. "She's sunk by now."

Gannon glared, nostrils pinched and white, lips bloodless. "Judas priest! How in hell do I manage to always hire such stupid sons of bitches? By Christ, if Dancey wasn't away on a freight run, I'd turn him loose on you. And you know what'd happen to you then. Anythin' you haven't told me?"

They shuffled their feet and Lobo murmured, "Laredo said to tell you he'll be seein' you from time to time. I dunno what he meant."

"He means he's gonna be hittin' Star Bar again, you dumb-ass." Gannon punched a fist into the palm of his other hand. "All right, we'll be ready for him! Double, no *triple* the nighthawks from now on. I want every inch of Star

Bar guarded from sundown to sun-up. You think you see or hear somethin' — *shoot*. Talk after. Now get the hell outa my sight."

When they had gone, he reached for a bottle of whiskey and a glass, but drank straight from the bottle. Yes sir, Laredo would be plumb loco to attack Star Bar now . . .

Trouble was, it was Gannon's saloon that burned down that night. In Sinola.

★ ★ ★

First they broke into Cheetham's Emporium, Mohawk using the blade of his Bowie knife to prise open a window.

Inside, guided by the old scout, Laredo took a half-empty box of dynamite, a long coil of fuse, a carton of fulminate detonators. While he was doing this, Mohawk emptied out a small nail keg as quietly as he could. He crabbed over to Laredo, showed him the inside of the cask.

"No good. Needs to be tarred."

"There's some gallon-size cans on yonder shelf." Mohawk moved to get one and a stubble brush. They each took ammunition to fit their weapons and Laredo scrawled an IOU on a scrap of wrapping paper by the cash drawer.

Mohawk grinned. "Gannon'll throw a fit."

They grabbed the grubsacks they had filled and slipped out into the night. While Laredo stuffed their loot into a sack and slung it behind his saddle, Mohawk went back inside and returned with two large bottles of coal oil.

This they poured over the back porch of the dark saloon and broke one wall. Laredo took half a stick of dynamite, slit it to take a detonator and fixed on a short length of fuse.

Mounted, Mohawk struck half-a-dozen vestas at once, walked his grey, dropping a flaring match every couple of feet, the last two going under the side wall.

The yard was lit-up with the flames that licked up the weathered timber, taking hold immediately.

They rode quickly on to Main where Laredo lit the fuse and hurled the dynamite against the batwings.

It blew almost instantaneously, slivers of wood whirring past them as they spurred down the street.

The explosion would wake the folk sleeping in the saloon and they would get out unharmed. But the fire already had such a hold that there would be little chance of saving the building . . .

They spurred away and Mohawk couldn't resist one resounding rebel yell that likely did more to stir the town than even the blast of the dynamite.

8

FAR to the south-west, the freight wagon rolled across drab plains, a slow beetle as seen from up on the butte known as Hawken's Leap.

Cougar sat his pinto, his battered rifle across his bare thighs, the heavy Le Mat pistol rammed into a belt above his breechclout. The red headband was tolerably new and clean and the dark, piercing eyes did not squint against the glare. He reached down idly to scratch at the top of the raw red scar that showed above his knee-high moccasins so favoured by the Chiracahua Apache and grunted a harsh syllable.

The ten warriors waiting at his back began to disperse immediately, wheeling away, five going down one side of the butte, five the other. Cougar sat there a little longer, then he spun his mount and took the eastern trail down, catching up with his band before they had reached the flats.

On the wagon, Dancey sat half-turned on the high seat, his Winchester in hand, hat brim tugged down low, but he still had to squint into the relentless glare. The man handling the reins as the heavy freighter rumbled and lurched over the rough trail towards the butte was called Hank Neeley and he wished Dancey hadn't picked him for this chore. He hated dealing with Indians and, although he would never admit it, this one who called himself Cougar made his bowels quake.

But Gannon paid fifty bucks extra so the money was worth the chance. Leastways, it was if a man got out still wearing his hair.

"They're comin'," Dancey said quietly. "Eleven. That'll be Cougar in the red headband."

Neeley wiped sweat from his face and swallowed, mouth suddenly parched.

Dancey grinned crookedly and nudged his shoulder roughly.

"Don't wet your pants, Hank. They won't touch us. Where else they gonna get their guns?"

The Indians had spread out on a rise across the trail where the sun-cracked boulders threw humpbacked shadows on the dry earth.

They stopped the wagon close to the biggest boulder, shielded from any prying army field glasses way back in the mountains. There were no greetings. The Indians parted and Cougar, his left arm seeming a trifle stiff, rode out, the butt of his '66 Winchester resting on his thigh now.

"How many?" he asked gruffly.

"Thirty," Dancey said, holding up both hands with fingers spread, pushing them towards the Apache three times.

Cougar grunted. A couple of his dog-faced warriors showed excitement.

Cougar untied a buckskin drawstring bag from his wooden saddle and tossed it to Dancey. "Gold."

Dancey checked and grinned when he looked up. "Good. This from the Tucson stage?"

Cougar ignored the question. "Show me guns."

Dancey climbed down. Hank Neeley sat stiffly holding the reins, sweat drenching his dusty clothes, inwardly writhing under the hard, impassive stares of the Apaches.

Cougar didn't dismount, walked his horse around to the side of the wagon. Three of his men went with him. Dancey snapped at Neeley to lend a hand and the man climbed down stiffly and together they removed the false side with the rifles fixed to the inside of the planks with leather straps. Cougar raised blazing eyes to Dancey's hard face.

"These not Winchesters!"

"No, not all. You got Henrys, couple Spencers, an Evans, Colt revolvin' rifles. They're all repeaters."

Cougar moved closer, slapped at the set of Colt revolving carbines. "These *old*! From your war! Long time to load."

"No — they been converted." Dancey unclipped one of the weapons, deftly removed the pin and held out the cylinder, holding it up so Cougar could see that it had been drilled through. "Originally cap-and-ball, loaded from the front. But she's been drilled-out and it'll take Henry rimfire cartridges now. Six shots. Good gun."

Cougar examined it, thrust it back. "Still old."

Dancey shrugged. "That's all I got. You want 'em?" He didn't like Cougar: the man was too iron-hard, no give in him at all. But he knew he was desperate for guns. He wanted to join Geronimo after he had finished on the Rim and in the Tonto Basin, and Geronimo didn't take anyone who couldn't bring his own repeating firearm these days.

Cougar's hatred for all whites showed plainly on his face and the nostrils of the big nose belled like a mustang's.

"We take. You got bullets?"

"Well — some." This was the tricky part, Dancey knew, and he felt sweat on his palm where he held his own rifle. "Not much — but I'll bring you plenty when you bring the rest of the gold."

"*Rest* of gold?" Cougar asked. "You say this enough."

"Oh, sure, it's enough for these guns and what little ammo we got, but, you see, Cougar, we gotta go to extra expense to get more ammo for you. And then — " Dancey tugged at an ear lobe, his heart hammering against his ribs. "Then there's the firin' pins."

Cougar frowned. "What these pins?"

Dancey grinned. *Ignorant Injun.* "Guns won't work without pins. Hammer hits the pin, drives it against the bullet case and then — bang! No pin, no bang."

"*This* one go bang!"

Cougar's rifle muzzle rammed up under Dancey's ear so suddenly that the big foreman lifted to tip-toe, sucking in a sharp breath through his teeth. He thought he was dead. His voice sounded womanish when he spoke.

"We don't get back in a certain time, the army'll be told of this rendezvous and they'll search till Doomsday to find your hideout, Cougar."

The Indian snarled and slammed the rifle barrel across the side of Dancey's head, dropping him to one knee. Neeley lifted his hands, eyes wide. One of the braves kicked his horse forward, used it to crush the man up against the wagon. Neeley collapsed to his hands and knees, head hanging, fighting for breath. Dancey shook his head, felt the blood trickling down his face as he glared through his pain at Cougar.

"No pins — no bang," he gasped.

The Apache's hatred was a tangible thing and Dancey's belly knotted but he tried not to let his fear show.

"It's easy. All you gotta do is hit the army payroll from Fort Winters. It'll be disguised as an army ambulance, movin' sick and wounded soldiers down to Fort Lowell at Tucson. No big escort. You can do it easy. You get us the gold, we get you the firing pins and ammo for these, and twenty good Winchesters. One a '73 for you."

Cougar's eyes sparked at this last. Even Geronimo would cut off his arm for a '73 Winchester, even if the weapon's legendary reputation really only applied to the special *one-of-a-thousand* guns handmade by the factory.

"Apache's don't scalp much, Dancey, but I wear yours on my belt one day!"

Dancey forced a grin. "I'll let my hair grow for you!"

★ ★ ★

Gannon was as jumpy as a bobcat with a tail full of ticks. He was *sure* that spreading his men out to guard every inch of his empire would be sufficient to keep the place safe from Laredo.

Instead, now he was down one

180

saloon, more than half of the feed-and-grain store next door, and had the threat of legal action from the livery for destruction of part of its stables and some livestock in the fire. Not to mention the ferry. Now the goddamn town was turning on him: fire in a timber town won no friends.

He'd had to redistribute his forces, which was likely exactly what Laredo wanted. *Why the hell hadn't the Mexes finished him!* Now he had men riding his line night and day, others stationed in Cheetham's Emporium, doubled-up guards at the cathouse in Powder Lane, two men with shot-guns waiting in the rear of the feed store — or what was left of it.

What the hell else could he do? Except go hunt down Laredo — and he wasn't yet prepared to lead his men into those hills where he was hiding out with old Mohawk.

Maybe he could do a deal with Cougar, have the Apache scour the hills for the Texan — after he had armed him with the repeater rifles he wanted so badly.

Yeah, he liked that idea . . . Laredo and Mohawk tortured at the hands of the Apaches. It cheered him up no end. He rode out of town and headed back to the ranch in a pretty good mood.

But it changed radically when he rounded the bend in the trail near the White Mountain turnoff.

There was smoke curling up over the ridge and it could only come from the hay pastures which he hadn't yet harvested for winter feed . . . a hell of a *lot* of smoke!

★ ★ ★

The fires in the winter feed pasture had done what Laredo wanted — drawn almost all of the men away from their stations. The smoke had looked mighty impressive, rolling and spreading high into the hot blue of the sky, able to be seen for miles. It had the look of a major fire — which it was, in all truth — and the men had automatically ridden to help extinguish it.

Laredo and Mohawk had watched them go from a timbered hill, ridden down through mesquite and rocks at one side of the lower waterfall and dismounted where the channel Gannon had dug for irrigation spilled into wooden-walled chutes. These carried water across a small valley, rising on heavy lodgepole stilts, snaking downwards to bring water to a series of fanned-out drains that would carry it on to the pastures that otherwise would not be able to be used for lack of grass growth. It was a vital link in Gannon's system.

They had painted the inside of the empty nail keg with tar and then Laredo had coiled fuse from the bottom to the top, fixing it to the keg's walls with small nails, bent over. Now Mohawk unloaded the keg from behind his saddle and Laredo took out the bundle of dynamite from his saddle-bags. He had a detonator with a short length of split fuse attached. He spliced this roughly to the fuse in the bottom of the keg, jammed in the board Mohawk had cut to hold the dynamite in place.

Laredo snapped a vesta on his thumbnail, touched it to the fuse, made sure it was burning properly, then hammered the prepared lid in place. He picked up the keg and dropped it into the swift-flowing water. It spun away. No smoke escaped as it bumped the sides of the chute and then floated swiftly down the zigzag system.

"There be enough air in that keg to keep the fuse burnin'?" asked Quade.

"Hope so. It always worked when we used it to blow up some Yankee weirs and break the ice on jammed rivers. Engineer who taught me used to be in the British Navy. Said he first learned underwater demolition off Alexandria when they had to recover some Egyptian prince's treasure."

"Well, you knowed what you were about the other times, so I guess this'll work, too."

Fifteen minutes later they had proof of that. There was a thundering explosion above the valley and splintered timber was flung wildly into the air. Only moments later there came the creak of splitting wood and the trestle supports of the chutes began to lean drunkenly as water gushed over the gap blasted in the system. A section of poles swung to the left, buckling in the middle, dragging yards of heavy wooden chutes down. Water sprayed and spilled everywhere. The falling poles set up a chain-reaction and the others fell swiftly, piling up untidily. Water roared out of the channel from the falls, flooding the valley and filling it with spreading muddy pools.

"By hell, old Gannon's sure gonna wish he'd give you back your land," opined Mohawk, shaking his head slowly.

"I'm working at persuading him," Laredo said quietly, looking at the destruction he had caused.

"Well, he's pretty dumb if he don't

get your message . . . oh-oh!"

Laredo straightened, turning around, ' Mohawk pointed back to the waterfall even as he spurred his grey forward.

A group of men thundered over the rise, the sun flashing from guns in their hands. Laredo's roan was moving almost at the grey's heels now and he heard the crack of the rifles.

Several puffs of dust rose from the ground ahead and to the sides of them. The fugitives zigged and zagged down into the valley.

Laredo's roan plunged down the steep slope, skidding on the wet grass. Mohawk's grey slipped sideways. The gunfire was more intense now, bullets zipping spitefully into the slope, a couple heating air past Laredo's head. He struggled to keep the roan upright. It was difficult and dangerous work. Gannon led his men recklessly down the same slope, guns hammering. Two horses went down and slid across in front of four more. There was a tangle of thrashing horse flesh and yelling men. But Gannon and three others came on, five more still mounted fighting to clear the sliding mass.

Laredo and Mohawk thundered across the valley, steering clear of the spreading mud and the splintered trestle timbers. Laredo unsheathed his Winchester and set the roan on a clear run down-valley, tripped in the saddle and pumped out seven shots.

He brought down two horses and the falling animals crashed into others nearby, bringing them down, too. It only left Gannon and one other man still riding. The rancher hadn't noticed his men go down, he was concentrating so hard on running down Laredo.

The other man realized they were out on their own, the men from the slope still sorting themselves out. He started to haul rein and Gannon became aware of it, snapped his head around to curse the man — and saw his own position.

Out ahead. On his own, facing Laredo.

He hauled rein abruptly, the horse protesting and tossing its head. Laredo's rifle whiplashed and Gannon went back over the horse's rump, hitting hard, limbs all a'tangle, the rifle dropping. Dazed, his left arm dangling, he stumbled to his feet and the other man rode in quickly to help him up on to his horse. Gannon yanked the man clear out of the saddle just as Laredo fired again.

The cowboy took the bullet meant for Gannon and it sent him sailing three feet to one side before crashing to the ground. By then Gannon was spurring back towards his other men who were at last surging forward. He ran in amongst them before wheeling and screaming orders to get after Laredo and Mohawk.

By then, the men were far away, running into the heavily-timbered hills where they could easily lose pursuit.

9

SHERIFF CLIFF LINDEEN squirmed in his chair behind his desk, wishing that Barr Gannon hadn't come storming into his office making his demands.

"Now how am I going to find this Texan and that old Indian scout, Mr Gannon?" the lawman asked with a whine in his voice. "I'm not even native to this country. You know it far better than me and you've just admitted you can't locate Laredo's hideout."

Gannon was in no mood for half-assed excuses and he leaned his big hands on the edge of the desk and glared down at the weak lawman.

"Cliff, I've done you favours — OK, OK, you haven't asked for 'em, but I've helped you out now and again — now it's time to square up and I'll have no backing-out!" He raised his voice, uncaring that the office door leading to the street was open. "Now you post a reward for Laredo and Mohawk, then you raise a posse and you get out into them hills and you damn well *find* 'em both!"

Lindeen was quaking inwardly but though he was a nervous type and actually afraid of Gannon, he had his share of pride. He had taken this badge and his salary was paid for by the town, not this brow-beating man who had almost everyone buffaloed. His voice shook but he stood up to the rancher.

"Mr Gannon, I appreciate whatever you've done for me and this community, but I know it's all been self-serving and if you'd just listen a minute, I could explain that the area where you claim Laredo is hiding out is across in the next county. I have no jurisdiction there."

Gannon all but threw up his hands. "Damnit, Lindeen, he's been committin' crimes in *this* county! I want him stopped before he wrecks Star Bar completely."

"Maybe you should have given him his share in the first place."

Lindeen wasn't sure where he found the courage to say that but he regretted it instantly and eased back in his chair when he saw Gannon's face as the man straightened.

The rancher glared down bitterly for a long minute and Lindeen began to sweat. "OK," Gannon said quietly, "I've tried to do this legal. You've refused to help and I've got enough pull in this dump to see you lose your badge over it — but that'll come later. I've got more important things to do right now."

He wheeled and strode to the door. Lindeen thrust to his feet.

"What're you going to do? Don't you . . . break the law."

Gannon paused and gave him a crooked smile, adjusting his hat. "Wouldn't dream of it."

Lindeen sat down slowly as the

man stormed away. He tugged at his ragged moustache, his heart hammering against his ribs. If he'd been a drinking man he'd have headed straight to the nearest saloon for a stiff whiskey.

Gannon was right, of course. Laredo's crimes had been committed in Three Peaks county. He should go after him. His mouth tightened.

He wasn't really suited to this job. He was too soft, cared too much for his family, didn't like being separated from them. He knew he should go out and try to find the Texan and Mohawk but it would mean leaving Urilla and young Queenie, and Urilla was keeping poorly again.

No, he wasn't suited to this job. He wanted to do it because his father and two brothers had been successful lawmen and he wanted to keep the family tradition going.

Of course, they were all dead now. Killed in the line of duty, every one of them. He was afraid he would be killed, too, never have a chance to see

Queenie grow up. Afraid . . .

Out on the street, Gannon paused at the corner of Powder Lane, glanced at his whorehouse as if making sure it hadn't been blown up or burned down, and lit a cheroot. As he shook out the match, he watched Dancey and Neeley bring in the freight wagon, both men startled by the sight of the charred remains of the saloon and the partially burned feed-and-grain store and livery stables.

He waved to Dancey who hauled rein and kicked on the brake bar. The foreman spoke to Neeley, told him to go get himself a drink, and the man needed no second telling.

Gannon stopped by the driver's seat. "I hope to hell you've got some good news for me."

Dancey knew better than to start asking questions about the saloon and so on when Gannon took that tone and looked the way he did.

"Well, Cougar didn't like it, holdin' back the firin' pins and ammo . . . "

"The hell with what he likes or don't like, is he gonna do it?"

Dancey nodded. "Yeah, he'll hit the payroll." The big foreman frowned. "Boss, you sure they only havin' a small escort? I mean, all that cash and only — how many? — seven men to guard it? Don't seem right."

"I pay plenty for important information," Gannon snapped, "and this man's never let me down. If he says only seven outriders, then that's what it'll be."

Dancey wasn't about to argue. "Don't tell me Laredo did all this." He gestured to the saloon ruins.

"What d'you think? I've just tried to prise Lindeen's ass off his desk chair but he's too fraidy-cat to mount a posse search in the hills. OK, I've tried to do it by the book. I like to cover myself because if ever a marshal or ranger came in here investigatin' just one thing I've done, it'd lead to others and then more, and pretty damn soon the whole operation'd be under investigation. But

I ain't gonna set back and twiddle my thumbs and wait to see what Laredo's gonna pull next."

Ward Dancey frowned. "Hell, we'd never find him in them hills, not with old Mohawk side-kickin' him. That old scout knows these hills better'n the 'Paches."

Gannon nodded, drawing deep on his cheroot. "Yeah, I know. So, if we can't get to Laredo, we'll make him come to us."

"What?"

Gannon smiled and Dancey saw that it was a genuine high-polish, show-the-teeth smile. The kind he gave when he was on top of a situation, boss man again, in complete control.

★ ★ ★

Cougar was glad of this chance to kill the yellow-leg soldiers. Any white-eye would do right now, but it would be especially good to kill these soldiers riding ahead and behind the lurching, canopied wagon that had the crossed sabres of the US Cavalry painted on the canvas.

Most of all, of course, he would like to kill Dancey. But he needed the man right now, needed him to get him the repeating rifles. And if he kept his word and brought Cougar one of the desired '73 Winchesters! *Agh!* He would be a big man, and even Geronimo himself would envy him.

But Cougar didn't feel that he could trust Dancey. This was the second time the man had lied to him. Withheld the firing pins this time, but previously he had brought only single-shot Trapdoor Springfields, with worn bores from years of use by the army instead of promised repeaters.

"You get us some gold we happen to know is bein' carried on the stage to Tucson and we'll bring you fifty repeaters," Dancey had said. "Winchesters."

The man had lied, of course. Now it was more gold, taken from the soldiers, before they delivered the Winchester rifles. Well, the gold would be easy and a true pleasure to steal . . . and once he had his own '73 Winchester in his hands, the first bullet through the barrel would have Ward Dancey's name on it.

He climbed down from the sun-hot rocks to where his small band waited and gave them orders. They would attack the wagon and sleepy soldiers from two sides. Kill one horse only to stop the wagon. They would need the other horses for the raids he was already planning, once he had the repeating rifles.

The warriors mounted and those designated to hit the wagon from the opposite side wheeled their painted mounts and started down the back of the ridge.

Cougar mounted his pinto with a leap, swept his arm out and around and the other five braves gave subdued war cries and started down the steep slope. *So few soldiers!* they thought. Cougar let them all get into position first before starting down himself, aiming his path so that he would cross that of the ambulance and the two lead outriders.

He stopped behind a large boulder, glanced up at the slope and saw a small amount of dust lift above a broken rock. The first group were in position. On the other slope there was another puff of dust, discernible only because he was looking for it. All was ready.

Sitting in the shadow of the boulder, he listened to the creak of harness, the jingle of chains, the rumble of iron-shod wheels over gravel as the wagon drew closer. Judging by the sound, he figured it was where he wanted it to be and heeled his pinto out into the middle of the trail, holding aloft his rifle with the eagle feather tied to the barrel, lending its spirit strength to the weapon so there would be good hunting — animals or men.

The lieutenant riding ahead with his sergeant saw the near-naked Indian walk his horse out from behind the boulder and he jerked back on his reins instantly, missing the curled lip of the old veteran sergeant, who had little use for West Pointers on their first tour of the West.

"My God, Sergeant, is that . . . an Apache?"

"Ain't just a 'Pache, Lieutenant, that's Cougar," the sergeant said, taking pleasure in seeing the blood drain from the lieutenant's face. He spat a stream of tobacco juice. "Want I should see what he wants?"

Even the shavetail lieutenant wasn't that green. "I don't think that'll be necessary, Sergeant," he said in clipped tones, his neatly trimmed golden moustache all but bristling. He had held his hand up as soon as he had halted and the wagon had stopped now, the rest of the escort fanning out, rifles ready, the men looking around.

The sergeant had given them their instructions before leaving Fort Winters.

"You do like I says," he'd told them.

"Never mind that Pointer. I'll get you through alive, just by followin' my instincts. The lieutenant, he'll foller the book — an' get us all killed."

The officer was already fighting indecision: should he charge straight ahead, pow-wow with Cougar, or . . . attack?

The decision was made for him. Cougar had hoped to hold their attention by revealing himself, while his men slipped quietly into position. But that grizzled sergeant had spoiled it.

His men, watching both sides of the trail as he had drilled into them, saw Cougar's men, five swarming down each slope, and a corporal shouted.

"They're hittin', Sarge! Both sides!"

The sergeant had already seen. The lieutenant had frozen, caught up in a web of indecision so the non-com took over, flinging his raised right arm forward.

"Hit the traces, Murphy, and keep goin' no matter what!"

It was the last order the sergeant ever

gave. Cougar's rifle spat flame and the man grunted, half twisted in his saddle and then fell sprawling in the dust. The lieutenant came alive on the instant, snatched at his sabre and charged Cougar even as the driver whipped up the wagon team. The officer yelled, holding the long curved blade straight ahead, shoulder level, on hard point, wrist and forearm teased as directed by the manual. He made a perfect, gallant figure for a painting. In fact, he might have stepped from several such paintings in the hallowed halls of the Point.

But he didn't get within ten feet of Cougar who casually shot him between the eyes and watched the man tumble from his horse, and fall beneath the hoofs of the thundering wagon that came racing along the trail much faster than Cougar expected.

He wheeled his pinto back behind the boulder as his men, screaming war cries now, closed in on both sides, the escort in the rear shooting but, strangely, dropping back, not trying to ride alongside the wagon as they usually did to protect its occupants.

Cougar grunted, startled, as he saw why when the canvas sides of the wagon were abruptly stripped away to reveal a mounted Gatling gun, crewed by the 'wounded' soldiers travelling in the ambulance.

Too late he understood why there had been so few soldiers guarding the payroll — if it was even in the wagon.

The big Gatling, recently approved by the War Department, was the Improved Version, fired at a faster rate, had larger vents although it still tended to clog with the filthy residue the black powder charge deposited. It stuttered as the gunner cranked the handle, also improved with gears to give a smoother traverse, and the iron barrels spun into position, fired, dropped away to make room for the next. Smoke enveloped the wagon as it thundered past the boulder where

Cougar sheltered. He saw two of his men smashed back into the landscape by the heavy calibre slugs. A horse went down, its neck shredded, throwing the rider. As he started to rise, the corporal raced in and decapitated him with a massive swing of the lieutenant's sabre he had recovered.

He saw his warriors hesitate, heeled his pinto into view, yelled encouragement. The gunner saw him, swung the Gatling's barrels towards him and Cougar crouched, wheeling the pinto back into the rocks. Boulders cracked and exploded under the hail of lead. A piece of sandstone lashed Cougar's cheek. He jumped the pinto for the shelter of some bigger rocks, felt the thud of lead in his side and swayed drunkenly, dropping his rifle, clutching wildly at his carved wooden saddle. Still, he straightened, pulled the Le Mat from his breechclout and fired off his last two rounds.

He hit the driver but although the man fell to his knees in front of the seat, he held on to the reins and then the Gatling sought Cougar again and he leapt the horse into shelter.

Peering between the rocks, left hand pressed into his bloody side, he saw his warriors cut down like a strong wind in the cornfield. Horses and men were blown all over the slopes, their blood splashing, soaking into the ground.

Then the wagon was past and the troopers galloped back to mutilate his men, hacking off ears and genitals for souvenirs.

Bleeding badly, stunned by the complete turn-around of events, Cougar rode deeper into the ridges, aware that the troopers would come after him once they had finished with his men.

They would never find him. No man would ever see him again — until he was ready to go to meet *Ysin*, the Apache god.

Then the white eyes would know of his going and remember it forever.

★ ★ ★

Laredo jerked up on the bunk, grabbing at his side as pain shot through his lower ribs.

"Damn, Mohawk, you'll have to change these bandages again. You've got 'em too tight or something."

Mohawk, coming off his bunk, Henry in hand, was making for the cabin door. "You keep 'em bound in place just as they are. That rib'll have a better chance to knit. Believe me."

Laredo doubted it, the way his side felt, like a rock was pressing on his lower ribs, but there was no time to discuss it now.

The same sound had wakened them both: a man's voice echoing through the canyons.

Mohawk was now crouched by the window, peering under the shutter.

"See anything?" Laredo asked, going to the door with his rifle, looking out through a crack in the warped planks.

"He ain't close. He's out there, but down in the big canyon, I'd say."

"Think I heard him earlier, but

farther off. Maybe he's working from canyon to canyon . . . what's he saying?"

"Can't make it out. We'll have to get up to the rim."

They took it easy, knowing it could be a trap. Whoever it was might have stumbled upon the canyon where their cabin was and be doing this so as to draw them out. Mohawk went ahead and crouched behind the low ridge of rocks past the corrals. Then, after a careful look around, Laredo followed, grimacing all the way as he moved in a crouch, side aching like hell. They waited, heard the voice again, bouncing up out of the big canyon still a hundred yards to their left. The words were too distorted to make out. Laredo jerked his head — they had to get to the rim.

Back to back, turning heads often, they made their way across their small hidden canyon, through the narrow entrance hidden in a boulderfield to the broken rim of the big canyon.

Each choosing a big rock for cover, they looked down and saw the lone rider with his horse standing ankle deep in the stream. The man had both hands cupped around his mouth, used his knees to turn his mount slowly as he called his message.

"We know you're in there somewheres, Laredo. You listen and listen good. We've got the gal and her old man. The Backmanns! We're holdin' 'em at Three Peaks and all you gotta do is show by sundown an' they won't be harmed." He paused and lowered his hands to spit and the fugitives saw that it was Ward Dancey.

"Gannon's had enough. He'll talk turkey with you, talk a deal. You've about ruined him an' he don't want Star Bar busted up no more. Come on in by sundown and he'll settle it."

"Sure — with a bullet between the eyes!" muttered Mohawk, starting to lift his rifle, but Laredo stopped him with sign.

Dancey was still calling. "The gal

an' her old man won't be harmed. Gannon tried to do this by the book but Lindeen wouldn't stick his neck out so he's gotta do it this way. Now, it's up to you whether the Backmanns live or die."

"An' the bastard says he wants to talk a deal!" Mohawk worked the Henry's lever but Laredo shook his head.

"No. Nailing Dancey won't help Teresa or Howard Backmann."

"If they got 'em like he says."

"We have to take his word, Mohawk."

The scout stared, frowning. "Man, you ain't thinkin' of goin' down there at sundown?"

Before he could answer, Dancey called once more. "By the way, we want Mohawk to come in, too. We don't aim for that old grizzly to be runnin' loose after we set up a deal with you, Laredo."

"Set up an ambush, more like!"

Laredo said nothing and Dancey repeated the entire message one more time, then rode out of the big canyon, much to Mohawk's disgust.

"We both owe that sonuver, Laredo!" he complained.

"I know. But we can't risk anything happening to Teresa." Laredo hitched himself into a more comfortable position, rubbing gently at the thick padding Mohawk had insisted on placing over his injured rib when he had changed the bandages after they first came to the hideout. "Got Gannon going, I guess."

He smiled ruefully and Mohawk spat in satisfaction. "Laredo, I sure don't want nothin' to happen to that gal or old Howard. They been good to me — I'll do whatever you say."

Laredo's eyes sought the leathery old face. "Even if it means riding in and giving ourselves up?"

Mohawk drew in a deep breath, nodded jerkily. "Even that. If there's no other way."

Laredo was silent for a time then said, "I don't see no other way right now. Except . . . "

Mohawk waited.

Laredo looked up and stopped rubbing his side.

He was smiling.

10

TERESA BACKMANN was worried about her father. He seemed a rugged man for his age on the outside, but she knew his heart was weak.

Doc Little had been treating him for months, had sent to New York for some new pills that were claimed to relieve the acute pain almost instantaneously. But, of course, like everything else in this damned isolated place, they hadn't yet arrived.

She knew that wasn't fair, taking out her frustration and anger on Three Peaks or the Mogollon Rim in general. She loved this place with its forests and rivers and waterfalls and lakes, distant peaks that never lost their caps of snow, wildlife abounding, clear, fresh air that had helped her father recover from the lung congestion that had almost killed him back in San Francisco. Her mother had died there of cholera when she was a small girl.

Yes, she loved this land. Too bad she couldn't say the same about the people who settled it.

Thank God they weren't all like Barr Gannon. Sitting on her ranch-house porch now, her father snoozing in his favourite canvas chair a few feet away, she stared down to the far end where Ward Dancey sat on the rail, smoking, boots propped against the house wall.

Gannon himself was inside somewhere, going through their account books with all the arrogance she had come to expect of the man. He had other men in the barn, at least one more in the bunkhouse where the Three Peaks' men were being held prisoner, too. She had been ordered to call them in from the range and they had been disarmed by Gannon's men, locked in the bunkhouse. They had been told they would be shot if they tried to leave for any reason whatever.

This enforced inactivity kept her blood boiling and she had already slapped Gannon's face. All that had earned her was a slap in return, an open-handed smack across the face that she still remembered in the ringing of her ears — and it had happened hours ago.

"You get somethin' through that pretty little head of yours, Teresa," Gannon had told her. "We're here until Laredo and that stinkin' old fool of a scout come in. They ain't here by sundown, why, we'll have to take steps to persuade 'em we mean business."

Frowning, rubbing her stinging face, she had asked, "What kind of steps?"

"Aw, I dunno. Nothin' too drastic. Might nail one of your pa's ears to a ponderosa at the start of that canyon country where I figure Laredo's hidin' out. Or" — and his grin had widened here and his eyes had sparked — "maybe we'll make it one of your ears. Or mebbe a finger . . ."

Sickened, she had run out on to the

porch to sit close to her father. Gannon was mad, but it was a dangerous kind of madness because the man was so arrogant, had such a monumental ego. He really believed he could do whatever he liked and get away with it. The thing was, any retribution, inevitable though it might be, wouldn't help her or her father if he had already mutilated them.

And it sure wouldn't help Laredo or old Mohawk.

"Riders comin', boss!"

The man who had been left in the hayloft called out and Dancey swung his legs down, flicking away his cigarette. He hurried into the house and came back with an anxious Gannon at his side. The rancher was buckling on his gun belt.

"The men know what to do?" he snapped.

"They been waitin' all afternoon for it," Dancey said, checking the loads in his pistol.

Gannon, ignoring Teresa and her

214

stirring father, stepped out into the yard, calling to the man in the hayloft.

"How many, Lobo?"

"Hell, looks like six or seven, boss!"

Gannon stiffened and Dancey paused thrusting his gun back into his holster. He glanced at Gannon who was frowning.

"The hell's that Texan tryin' to pull?" He rounded on Teresa. "You got more of your crew out you ain't told us about?"

"You know all my crew's in the bunkhouse," she told him curtly, helping Howard Backmann out of the chair.

"See who it is, Lobo?" called Dancey.

"Judas, yeah! It . . . you ain't gonna believe this! It's Lindeen — and looks like he's got a posse with him."

"Lindeen!" spat Gannon. "What in the name of hell . . . ?"

They could see the dust cloud rising now against the afternoon sun, giving it a dull brassy look. The lines of riders moved purposefully below it, coming straight in for the Three Peaks' gate.

"What we gonna do?" Dancey asked quietly.

"Stay put." Gannon swung towards Teresa and her father. "You two keep your mouths shut. We're here because you asked us to come over — back you up in case Laredo hit your place like he hit mine."

"Who'll believe that!" she scoffed.

"You *make* Lindeen believe it . . . or sometime this ranch house is gonna burn down around your pretty little ears. You savvy?"

"Who the hell d'you think you are, Gannon?" demanded Howard Backmann, chest heaving with emotion. "What you need is to have your legs kicked out from under you and Laredo's the man to do it. Why, if he . . . "

"Shut up, old man!" snapped Gannon, watching as Lindeen led his posse through the gate into the ranch yard. He spoke through his teeth. "You just

216

remember what I said!"

Teresa took her father's arm, holding tightly to it, afraid he might try something and be hurt.

Sheriff Lindeen reined down some yards away from where the group stood on the porch, the men with him fanning out. They all carried firearms, four with rifles, two with shot-guns, and they were all townsmen.

And they all looked mighty grim, even if a couple did seem pretty uncertain now they were facing Gannon.

Gannon greeted Lindeen affably enough but the sheriff ignored him, asked the Backmanns if they were all right, though he had to clear his throat twice first. Only after Teresa assured him she and her father were unharmed, did he turn his gaze to Barr Gannon and Dancey who stood at his side with a look of half-amusement on his face.

"Mr Gannon, I believe you have been holding the Backmanns hostage here on their own ranch."

"What the hell're you talkin' about?"

Gannon demanded.

"Judas, they *asked* us," put in Dancey. "Scared that crazy damn Texan an' that old scout were gonna hit their spread like they hit Star Bar."

"Oh?" Lindeen moved his gaze briefly to Dancey then on to Teresa. "I don't think I'll even bother asking Miss Backmann if that's correct. You see, Mr Gannon, what I've been told is that you've been holding the Backmanns hostage in order to bring Laredo and Mohawk Quade out of hiding because you want revenge on them for what they've done to your ranch."

"You're loco." There was scorn in the rancher's voice but his face was wary now. "If you'd taken your damn posse up into the canyon country and searched for them two maniacs, we mightn't be livin' in fear right now of what they're gonna do next."

"Oh, I wouldn't worry about that."

"No, well you don't have a ranch worth a couple of hundred thousand to worry about. If you did . . . "

"I wouldn't worry about it, Mr Gannon," cut in Lindeen, the sweat sheening his face now, but he was determined to say what he came to say no matter how scared he was. "I wouldn't worry about it because Laredo and Mohawk Quade are locked up safe in my jail in town." Into the stunned silence, he added. "They rode in and gave themselves up, so there's no need for hostages now. You will turn the Backmanns loose, Mr Gannon, and if they want to press charges against you for deprivation of liberty I will be happy for them to follow it through to prosecution."

"Why, you miserable, two-bit, yeller-backed son of a bitch!"

Gannon stopped as four rifles and two shotguns swung down to cover him.

"These are townsmen who have had enough of your roughshod tactics, Mr Gannon — Laredo and Mohawk Quade may have broken the law, too, but they've inspired the town to stand up to you and your arrogance." He spoke to the smiling girl and her father. "I'd be obliged if you'd accompany us back to town, ma'am ... and, of course, you, too, Mr Gannon — with your men."

* * *

"I reckon we could change them bandages on your ribs now."

Sitting on the edge of the bunk in the jail cell, Laredo looked up, glanced out into the passage where the guard Lindeen had left was seated at a desk, boots up, reading a ragged copy of the Tombstone *Epitaph*.

"Yeah, well it's about time. This side is giving me hell. It's days since the bandage was changed and folk are starting to stand upwind of me."

In point of fact, it was less than six hours since Mohawk had changed the bandage, but Laredo stretched out on the bunk now, hiking up his buckskin shirt and Mohawk moved across and

220

started to unwind the cloth.

The guard glanced across. "What you doin'?"

"His ribs are troublin' him. Doc Little said to leave the bandage on for a few days. Well, time's up, and he ain't gettin' any better. If we're gonna be waitin' here for a trial, we might as well get him some medical attention."

"You'll have to ask Lindeen about that," the man said and returned to his paper. But he snapped his head up a few minutes later when Mohawk stepped back from Laredo's bunk and exclaimed, "Judas! Man, no wonder it's been givin' you hell! End of the rib's comin' through the skin. Hey, Deputy, take a look at this."

The guard came across, curious, and Mohawk stepped to one side as he halted at the bars so he could see — see the twin-barrelled derringer held in Laredo's hand, the same one Mohawk had hidden amongst the bandages earlier back up at their cabin.

"Two ·41 calibre shots, Deputy," Laredo told the startled man as he swung his legs off the bunk and came to the bars. "No, don't move away! Stay put and reach down those keys and unlock the door — after you hand your six-gun to Mohawk."

The man was pale, a townsman recruited for the job. His hand shook some as he handed over his gun to Quade and then he unlocked the door and stepped inside at Laredo's invitation.

"Why the hell you fellers give yourself up if you wanted to break out again?"

"The idea was to meet Gannon's deadline without getting ourselves killed. Once Lindeen has turned loose the Backmanns, there's no need for us to make sitting targets of ourselves."

"Hell, Lindeen wouldn't allow that. He's weak, but he's a stickler for the law."

"Well, you congratulate him for us."

They took the man's gunbelt and locked him in and, as they started away

222

he said, "Hand me in the paper before you go, huh? Gimme somethin' to do while I'm waitin'."

* * *

There was still light when Lindeen returned with his posse and the Star Bar crew. But something had changed since they had ridden out of Three Peaks.

The Backmanns were there with them, but it was obvious that Gannon's men had taken over along the trail to town. The posse men, angry townsmen, were no match for the hardcases employed by Star Bar and before they had left Three Peaks a mile behind, Gannon's crew were in charge. Lindeen was pale and crestfallen — his one attempt at really doing his job appeared to have ended in failure.

"Don't worry, Cliff," Gannon had told him after his men had disarmed the posse men. "We'll see that justice is done — our way."

223

"I sent for the Arizona Rangers," the sheriff said, his words rocking the Star Bar men. "I don't have enough experience to handle someone like you."

"Well, you can send off another wire and cancel 'em," Gannon said. "But first, let's take care of Laredo and Mohawk Quade." He turned towards Lobo and the Mexican, Quintana. "You two take the Backmanns down to Dora at the cathouse and keep 'em there till I tell you different."

"You're crazy, Gannon, plumb crazy," said Howard Backmann in a feeble show of resistance.

Gannon smiled. "Better watch your mouth, Howard. You might be talkin' to your future son-in-law."

Backmann's eyes widened and Teresa, dismounting, froze, one foot still in the stirrup, stunned. "I'll never marry you, Barr Gannon!"

He shrugged. "Just a thought — but we'll talk about it later." He jerked his head and Lobo moved in, took her arm and led her away, the Mexican following with Howard.

Gannon told the crestfallen posse men to go back to their families and think themselves lucky. Gun in hand, he led Lindeen into the law office, followed by Dancey and more of his men. It took but a few moments to learn that Laredo and Mohawk were no longer there.

Gannon swore and looked mad enough to straighten horseshoes with his teeth. Lindeen seemed nervous, but pleased at the escape. He picked up a yellow telegraph form off his desk that had apparently been delivered while he was out of town. He glanced up quickly.

"My God, the Apaches are loose!" That got everyone's attention. "Says here Cougar and some of his men tried to rob an army payroll wagon but were driven off by a Gatling gun. Cougar got away but they don't know how many men he has with him."

Dancey swore aloud, looking at

Gannon. "Just what we need," growled the rancher. "All right, start scourin' the town. You see either Laredo or Mohawk, shoot on sight."

He locked Lindeen and the deputy in the cells and went outside with Dancey just as there was a racket of gunfire from Powder Lane where the Backmanns had been taken. Gannon started running, Dancey at his heels.

Laredo saw Lobo and the Mexican bringing the Backmanns towards the lane and he knew where Gannon was going to stash them while he hunted them down. He had suspected that Gannon might easily turn the tables on Lindeen and hadn't aimed to be sitting like a clay pigeon in a jail cell when he arrived back in town.

Now, rifle in hand, he slipped behind the charred ruins of the saloon and cut through the yard of the half-deserted feed-and-grain store to Powder Lane. There were some shouts and laughter coming from the cathouse, winding-up for the night to come, but otherwise the town seemed subdued, as if waiting for something.

Mohawk was up on the roof of the saloon on the opposite side of the street with his Henry and while he may have seen the Backmanns, he could not see into Powder Lane from his position. So it was up to Laredo and he didn't hesitate, stepped out of the shadow of a leaning wall, Winchester braced into his hip.

Teresa gasped his name as they stopped dead and then Lobo was reaching for the girl, to drag her in front of him. The Mexican thrust Howard Backmann roughly into the wall of a frame building as his six-gun came up blasting. The lead fanned Laredo's face and he dropped, rolling, shooting across his body, levering, shooting again. Quintana crashed into the wall, bleeding, his gun sagging. Backmann snatched it out of the man's hand and he pushed the muzzle into the big body and pulled the trigger.

Lobo was wild-eyed at seeing his

pard go down and he snapped a shot at Laredo as he backed out of the lane, dragging the struggling girl with him.

"I'll kill her, so help me I will!"

He started to lift his gun towards her and she grabbed his hand sank her teeth into his wrist. He yelled, twisted a hand in her hair and instinctively flung her from him. An instant later he was dead, blasted backwards into the street by Laredo's rifle.

The Texan steadied the girl, thrust her towards her father. "Stay down! Get under cover somewhere!"

He didn't wait for her reply as Mohawk opened up from the roof with his Henry. Laredo crouched by the building on the corner of the lane, saw Gannon's men scattering, one down in the street, writhing. Gannon had spotted Mohawk, snapped two fast shots at the false front. Laredo dived out into the street, six-gun in one hand, rifle in the other, both blazing. He dropped the rifle after firing it, but kept triggering the Smith and Wesson. Two men staggered, one falling after taking several paces, coughing blood. Mohawk's Henry was thundering as bullets kicked gravel all around Laredo's rolling body. He crouched behind a horse trough, snapped a shot at Gannon, missed, looked for Dancey, saw the man running, doubled-over, along the walk, grasping a shotgun. He fired and Dancey gave him one barrel, the shot splintering the trough, drenching him with water, slivers of wood stinging him. He ducked and the second barrel thundered and when he looked up cautiously, he went cold.

A hole had been blasted in the flimsy false front and Mohawk's broken body was rolling across the street awning roof. It fell with a thud, unmoving. Laredo rammed his pistol into his holster, dived for his rifle, scooping it up and spinning around as Gannon stepped out only yards away, teeth bared, running forward, shooting, certain of his target.

A red streak flashed across Laredo's face as he came up to one knee, lever and trigger working, hammering four bullets into Gannon, the man's body twisting and spinning before spilling to the street. A slug punched dust from the shoulder of his shirt and he spun, saw Dancey, brought up the rifle and squeezed the trigger.

The hammer fell on an empty chamber. He flung the weapon aside, snatched his pistol and blazed a shot at Dancey who was diving into an alley. Splinters flew and Laredo leapt up, running, shooting again. But it was the last shot in the gun and he slammed against the wall, reloading with shaking fingers, but even as he thumbed home the final cartridge, he heard the rapid thunder of retreating hoofbeats.

Teresa ran towards him and flung her arms about him and he made to thrust her aside, but saw that it was almost full dark now. Dancey would make good his escape.

Mohawk was dead, as was Gannon

and three of his men. Howard Backmann, answering his daughter's concerned query, said he'd never felt better in his life.

"By Godfrey, you've sure shook up this town since you returned, Laredo," the old man said.

Laredo nodded. "All I wanted was my land . . . all Mohawk wanted was to set out his days in peace, not pieces."

"Oh, Laredo, don't!" Teresa's grip tightened on his arm. "It's . . . terrible but, well, it's all over now."

"No. Not till Dancey's dead."

She stared up into his face, eyes searching the hard, rugged lines; this man who displayed no outward softness, only the tough gauntness of a man who lived a life that had treated him less than kindly, but had not bent him in any way.

"When will you leave?" she asked quietly, and his gaze sharpened, knowing here was a woman to hold on to, one who savvied a man had certain self-imposed codes and that he had to live up to those codes no matter what.

"In the morning," he said.

"I'll wait for you at Three Peaks."

No tears, no pleading, just the confidence that he would do what he had to and then return to her.

★ ★ ★

He tracked Ward Dancey into the canyon country and stayed on his trail for two days without sighting the man. Then he saw him on a high trail back of Hawken's Leap, and he dismounted, unsheathed the Winchester, and took a steady bead.

The bullet clipped the sandstone rock not six inches from Dancey and the man almost fell off the rim in fright. But he recovered fast, hammered five shots down at Laredo. When the echoes had died away, slapping from wall to wall of the snaking canyons, the roan lay thrashing in a welter of blood. Laredo headshot it out of its misery, triggered at Dancey but the man was gone now.

"Hope you've got a good pair of boots, Laredo!" the mocking voice called.

Laredo slung his canteen, saddlebags full of grub and spare ammunition over his left shoulder and, rifle in his right hand, began the long climb up to the trail above.

The heat beat at him and three times loose rocks gave way under his grip and he slid back several feet. Doggedly, he started up again. He paused, thought he heard a wild cry, but then saw the wheeling hawk and figured it must have been the bird.

He made it to a ledge below where he had seen Dancey, rested to get his breath and wipe the sweat out of his eyes.

He jumped when there was a whoosh and a thud and he stared incredulously at the crude lance quivering in the ledge.

There was a fresh scalp tied to the

butt, still dripping blood, the hair easily recognizable.

Dancey's scalp.

Backing carefully, rifle at the ready, Laredo moved to where he could look up to the trail. But it was empty. Above the trail, on the rim itself, was a horseman astride a painted pinto, a bloody rag tied over a wound in his left side with rawhide. The Apache stared solemnly at the Texan, lifted a hand in brief salute, then turned and rode slowly out of sight.

No words had been exchanged, but Laredo knew a debt had been repaid.

Later, he began the long walk back to Three Peaks.

THE END

Other titles in the
Linford Western Library:

TOP HAND
Wade Everett

The Broken T was big. But no ranch is big enough to let a man hide from himself.

GUN WOLVES OF LOBO BASIN
Lee Floren

The Feud was a blood debt. When Smoke Talbot found the outlaws who gunned down his folks he aimed to nail their hide to the barn door.

SHOTGUN SHARKEY
Marshall Grover

The westbound coach carrying the indomitable Larry and Stretch headed for a shooting showdown.

FIGHTING RAMROD
Charles N. Heckelmann

Most men would have cut their losses, but Frazer counted the bullets in his guns and said he'd soak the range in blood before he'd give up another inch of what was his.

LONE GUN
Eric Allen

Smoke Blackbird had been away too long. The Lequires had seized the Blackbird farm, forcing the Indians and settlers off, and no one seemed willing to fight! He had to fight alone.

THE THIRD RIDER
Barry Cord

Mel Rawlins wasn't going to let anything stand in his way. His father was murdered, his two brothers gone. Now Mel rode for vengeance.

ARIZONA DRIFTERS
W. C. Tuttle

When drifting Dutton and Lonnie Steelman decide to become partners they find that they have a common enemy in the formidable Thurston brothers.

TOMBSTONE
Matt Braun

Wells Fargo paid Luke Starbuck to outgun the silver-thieving stagecoach gang at Tombstone. Before long Luke can see the only thing bearing fruit in this eldorado will be the gallows tree.

HIGH BORDER RIDERS
Lee Floren

Buckshot McKee and Tortilla Joe cut the trail of a border tough who was running Mexican beef into Texas. They stopped the smuggler in his tracks.

BRETT RANDALL, GAMBLER
E. B. Mann

Larry Day had the choice of running away from the law or of assuming a dead man's place. No matter what he decided he was bound to end up dead.

THE GUNSHARP
William R. Cox

The Eggerleys weren't very smart. They trained their sights on Will Carney and Arizona's biggest blood bath began.

THE DEPUTY OF SAN RIANO
Lawrence A. Keating and
Al. P. Nelson

When a man fell dead from his horse, Ed Grant was spotted riding away from the scene. The deputy sheriff rode out after him and came up against everything from gunfire to dynamite.

FARGO: MASSACRE RIVER
John Benteen

The ambushers up ahead had now blocked the road. Fargo's convoy was a jumble, a perfect target for the insurgents' weapons!

SUNDANCE: DEATH IN THE LAVA
John Benteen

The Modoc's captured the wagon train and its cargo of gold. But now the halfbreed they called Sundance was going after it . . .

HARSH RECKONING
Phil Ketchum

Five years of keeping himself alive in a brutal prison had made Brand tough and careless about who he gunned down . . .

FARGO: PANAMA GOLD
John Benteen

With foreign money behind him, Buckner was going to destroy the Panama Canal before it could be completed. Fargo's job was to stop Buckner.

FARGO: THE SHARPSHOOTERS
John Benteen

The Canfield clan, thirty strong were raising hell in Texas. Fargo was tough enough to hold his own against the whole clan.

PISTOL LAW
Paul Evan Lehman

Lance Jones came back to Mustang for just one thing — revenge! Revenge on the people who had him thrown in jail.

HELL RIDERS
Steve Mensing

Wade Walker's kid brother, Duane, was locked up in the Silver City jail facing a rope at dawn. Wade was a ruthless outlaw, but he was smart, and he had vowed to have his brother out of jail before morning!

DESERT OF THE DAMNED
Nelson Nye

The law was after him for the murder of a marshal — a murder he didn't commit. Breen was after him for revenge — and Breen wouldn't stop at anything . . . blackmail, a frameup . . . or murder.

DAY OF THE COMANCHEROS
Steven C. Lawrence

Their very name struck terror into men's hearts — the Comancheros, a savage army of cutthroats who swept across Texas, leaving behind a bloodstained trail of robbery and murder.

SUNDANCE: SILENT ENEMY
John Benteen

A lone crazed Cheyenne was on a personal war path. They needed to pit one man against one crazed Indian. That man was Sundance.

LASSITER
Jack Slade

Lassiter wasn't the kind of man to listen to reason. Cross him once and he'll hold a grudge for years to come — if he let you live that long.

LAST STAGE TO GOMORRAH
Barry Cord

Jeff Carter, tough ex-riverboat gambler, now had himself a horse ranch that kept him free from gunfights and card games. Until Sturvesant of Wells Fargo showed up.

McALLISTER ON THE COMANCHE CROSSING
Matt Chisholm

The Comanche, McAllister owes them a life — and the trail is soaked with the blood of the men who had tried to outrun them before.

QUICK-TRIGGER COUNTRY
Clem Colt

Turkey Red hooked up with Curly Bill Graham's outlaw crew. But wholesale murder was out of Turk's line, so when range war flared he bucked the whole border gang alone . . .

CAMPAIGNING
Jim Miller

Ambushed on the Santa Fe trail, Sean Callahan is saved by two Indian strangers. But there'll be more lead and arrows flying before the band join Kit Carson against the Comanches.

GUNSLINGER'S RANGE
Jackson Cole

Three escaped convicts are out for revenge. They won't rest until they put a bullet through the head of the dirty snake who locked them behind bars.

RUSTLER'S TRAIL
Lee Floren

Jim Carlin knew he would have to stand up and fight because he had staked his claim right in the middle of Big Ike Outland's best grass.

THE TRUTH ABOUT SNAKE RIDGE
Marshall Grover

The troubleshooters came to San Cristobal to help the needy. For Larry and Stretch the turmoil began with a brawl and then an ambush.

WOLF DOG RANGE
Lee Floren

Will Ardery would stop at nothing, unless something stopped him first — like a bullet from Pete Manly's gun.

DEVIL'S DINERO
Marshall Grover

Plagued by remorse, a rich old reprobate hired the Texas Troubleshooters to deliver a fortune in greenbacks to each of his victims.

GUNS OF FURY
Ernest Haycox

Dane Starr, alias Dan Smith, wanted to close the door on his past and hang up his guns, but people wouldn't let him.

DONOVAN
Elmer Kelton

Donovan was supposed to be dead. Uncle Joe Vickers had fired off both barrels of a shotgun into the vicious outlaw's face as he was escaping from jail. Now Uncle Joe had been shot — in just the same way.

CODE OF THE GUN
Gordon D. Shirreffs

MacLean came riding home, with saddle tramp written all over him, but sewn in his shirt-lining was an Arizona Ranger's star.

GAMBLER'S GUN LUCK
Brett Austen

Gamblers seldom live long. Parker was a hell of a gambler. It was his life — or his death . . .

ORPHAN'S PREFERRED
Jim Miller

Sean Callahan answers the call of the Pony Express and fights Indians and outlaws to get the mail through.

DAY OF THE BUZZARD
T. V. Olsen

All Val Penmark cared about was getting the men who killed his wife.

THE MANHUNTER
Gordon D. Shirreffs

Lee Kershaw knew that every Rurale in the territory was on the lookout for him. But the offer of $5,000 in gold to find five small pieces of leather was too good to turn down.

RIFLES ON THE RANGE
Lee Floren

Doc Mike and the farmer stood there alone between Smith and Watson. There was this moment of stillness, and then the roar would start. And somebody would die . . .

HARTIGAN
Marshall Grover

Hartigan had come to Cornerstone to die. He chose the time and the place, and Main Street became a battlefield.

SUNDANCE: OVERKILL
John Benteen

When a wealthy banker's daughter was kidnapped by the Cheyenne, he offered Sundance $10,000 to rescue the girl.